# The Eighth Dwarf

R.A. GOLI

# The Eighth Dwarf

R.A. GOLI

EPIC
PUBLISHING

# CHAPTER ONE

TIBERIUS WIPED the sweat from his brow and stood, then stretched and grimaced at the dull ache in his back. The front door of his shared cabin slammed shut. He heard whistling and footsteps from the other dwarves before he saw them. Resting his hammer against the anvil, he swallowed a mouthful of ale, then stared out of the workshop as men passed, picks over shoulders, on their way to the mines. A couple of them turned his way and smiled or waved, Tiberius nodded back. When the men were out of sight, he cleared his throat and spat. His resentment had been growing over the last few months. He was talented. It was an art, what he did. He crafted weapons and armor with mastery, each piece unique, exquisite, and virtually unbreakable. Customers came from miles around to commission his work, and his pieces fetched a hefty amount of gold.

Split between the eight of them, the spoils didn't seem so grand. Tiberius felt he deserved the biggest cut since he was the most capable and creative, but the dwarves lived in a democracy, and everything was equal. Which is why he slept in a single bed in a shared room within a meager cottage, instead of in his own cottage, or better yet, a manor home. Closer to the capital, perhaps. Closer to the excitement. Anything would be better than living this way—no privacy, too noisy and smelly, as though he were a child living with siblings instead of a grown man on his own—but other forces had conspired against him in that regard.

Years ago, residents of the forest started complaining about an overcrowding problem with far too many cottages being built. In response, the king put a moratorium on new buildings, so when Tiberius set out on his own, he found a shortage of real estate and was forced to search for shared housing. His experience was less than favorable. The first "Roommates Wanted" sign he answered turned out to be a beautiful and lonely young woman, but the only way to enter the residence was by climbing a hair-ladder—very inconvenient—and the woman's mother was an absolute crone.

So, Tiberius moved in with an old lady in a quieter part of the forest. She seemed sweet at first but was always trying to lure children into the house, and there was a pervasive smell of gingerbread and a persistent ant problem. That was when he moved in with the dwarves. There were far too many of them, and they were ridiculously cheerful—always singing and whistling—but after what he had been through with previous roommates, they seemed the most normal.

The way Tiberius saw it, he was a craftsman, an artist; the others were just laborers. Of course, they would have argued it was they who did all the difficult work, complaining about the tough conditions in the mines: the dust, the lack of light. Tiberius didn't buy it. His labors were just as physical, and he knew the others enjoyed their work in the mines, always whistling and skipping.

He picked up his hammer and imagined one of their faces in the shining metal that sat on the anvil. Klaus, maybe. Or Graymont. Yes, him, with his ruddy cheeks and smiling face.

*CLANG.*

He would wipe that cheerful expression away.

*THWACK.*

Tiberius worked with a renewed vigor well into the afternoon.

~

TIBERIUS WAS EXITING the bath when he heard the whistling. He always washed before the others finished work. It took a lot of effort to fill and heat the tub eight times and some of the dwarves didn't bother; there was no way he was bathing after the miners. What would be the point? He would come out dirtier than he was when he went in.

He dressed hurriedly, wanting to leave for his evening walk before someone roped him into helping with chores. It was his turn to do the dishes, which he accepted, but he didn't feel the need to do more than that. Washing the dishes after eight dwarves, who were more like pigs at a trough than men, would take him two hours, at least. He tied his boots, grabbed his satchel, and headed out.

A few of the men were gathered in the kitchen, awaiting their turn to bathe or preparing vegetables for dinner. "Going for your walk, Tiberius," Morom said, his dirty face split into a knowing grin.

"Indeed." Tiberius returned the smile. *Idiot.* The fact that he went for a walk every night didn't stop Morom from also asking every night. He would often call him *Moron* to see if the daft prick would notice. He never did. "Well, be back for dinner," Morom said.

"And dishes," Brok added with an obnoxious laugh.

Tiberius smiled, turned on his heel, and headed towards the forest. His walks initially started as a way to escape the hustle, bustle, and stink of a house filled with eight men and their dirty, sweaty bodies. He would find a secluded spot, pull out his pipe and tobacco pouch, smoke, and watch the moon and stars. An hour or two leaning against a broad oak, watching the approach of night through the lush canopy, would do wonders for his temperament.

~

LATER, as he washed dishes, he strained to hear what the other men were talking about at the dining table. Normally, they were plenty loud, but now they spoke in muted tones. Finally, his curiosity won over his desire to finish the task.

"What are you gossiping about?"

The seven of them quieted and looked at Tiberius as he approached, dishrag in hand.

"Well?"

Klaus cleared his throat, then looked around the table. A few of the others nodded.

"We found something," he said. "In the mines."

Tiberius's eyes widened as his mind raced. *What have they found? A dragon's lair, a dead body?* "Well, what is it?"

Klaus slid a hand into his pocket and produced a gem. Tiberius took the stone and studied it. Hard and perfectly clear, it didn't look like any he had ever seen. Somehow, it seemed even brighter than a diamond.

"It almost looks like glass, but we don't mine glass. It's definitely not a diamond. We're not sure what it is," Klaus said.

"Very curious." He held it up to the sconce. "Were you planning on keeping this from me?"

"We didn't want you to get excited. We think it could be worth a lot."

Tiberius smiled—a rare, genuine smile that reached his eyes. The thought of riches had that effect on him. "A newly discovered gem could be worth much. Is there more?"

"There's plenty," said Brok.

"We thought you could use it to adorn the swords and shields you make. It is striking; it may increase their value. Or perhaps finer items like a lady's hair comb or something," said Klaus.

"Bring more." Tiberius pocketed the prize and returned to the dishes.

OVER THE NEXT FEW MONTHS, they brought copious amounts, which they piled in his work shed. Tiberius tried to manipulate it into armor or weaponry, but it wouldn't melt. He couldn't smash it with his hammer; it refused to yield under any pressure, and no weapon he owned would cut it. After weeks of trying, he was frustrated. They had a pile of the material, but if he couldn't turn it into something useful, it'd be worthless—a pretty gem to adorn a lady's trinket box, perhaps, but nothing more.

# CHAPTER TWO

Tiberius trudged into the forest, his mood more sour than usual. The discovery of the gem, which they were calling glasz, had excited him. He had believed he had found his way out of this squalor. Even split eight ways—he supposed he would have to give the other men a finder's fee at least—he foresaw great riches and perhaps even a small amount of fame, which brought with it many rewards: women, food, ale. What more did a man need? If he couldn't morph it into something useful, he would be stuck in his humble cottage with his annoying companions. The other dwarves didn't have the skills to make the glasz into anything useful, and they hadn't seemed perturbed by the anticipated loss of coin. They were happy with things as they were. They talked about having a roof over their heads and full bellies as though that was all life had to offer. Tiberius wanted more. He deserved more!

He stomped between trees, his heavy boots crushing twigs and leaves. So self-absorbed was he, he didn't notice the sky darken; a cluster of grey clouds swiftly covering the moon. It was only when he stumbled on a root and crashed face-first into the dirt, his hands splayed out in front of him, that he looked around.

He sat up and wiped his hands as he scanned the forest. He saw nothing unusual besides the fact it was so gloomy. Even as he sat, the darkness increased, the air thick and oppressive. He stood, brushed off his clothing, and cautiously continued his journey, searching for the small clearing with the uprooted stump he claimed as his smoking place.

As he approached, weaving between the oaks, birch, and maple trees, the cloud cover over the moon dissipated, and the celestial orb shone brighter than he had ever witnessed. He gasped, leaning against a nearby fir as he watched the moonbeams collimate, forming a singular, shining beam.

He ran deeper into the woods, desperate to see what could cause such an unnatural occurrence.

"Goblin's balls," he said when he reached the edge of the clearing.

There was a woman standing in the middle of the open space, clasping a round object, arm raised as though what she held was a sacrifice to the sky. The moon's rays shot directly into both the object and the woman, illuminating the ground around her. Tiberius had only ever seen mere parlor tricks; he had never seen anyone command the moon.

Tiberius watched, half hidden behind the trunk of an oak, as the bright light pulsed, then disappeared. Then the witch collapsed.

With no consideration for his safety, he rushed forward, then knelt beside her still body. He could see clearly now, the moonlight having returned to the comforting glow of an ordinary night. The woman was beautiful. Her porcelain skin was smooth and fragile, as though it would shatter at the slightest touch. Her expression was serene, and her long, dark hair fanned out across her breasts, firm and perfect, rising and falling with each breath.

He moved his hand to her chest and slid her hair away so he might have a better view of the cleavage that spilled from the top of her corset.

"Get away from me, you pervert," she said, and Tiberius felt the sting of her hand across his cheek. She sat up, and he crawled backwards.

"I'm sorry, I was just seeing if you were alright."

She raised an eyebrow at him and then started searching the ground.

"Where is it? Where's the apple?" she said, her agitation increasing.

He looked and saw the blackened orb resting in a tuft of grass behind him. He scrambled to his feet, towards the orb, grabbed it, and turned to face her.

"You mean this?" he asked as he tossed it in the air.

She stood, her eyes narrowed, arm outstretched.

"Give it to me, little man," she said.

Tiberius laughed. "Little man? Don't be fooled by my stature. I'm more man than you could handle." He grabbed his crotch with his free hand and squeezed as he blew her a kiss. He was surprised when she laughed.

"What's the apple for?" he asked.

"Just give it to me."

"Not until you tell me."

She sighed, walked towards the edge of the clearing, and sat on his smoking stump. "Fine. I'm not up to traveling yet anyway and what harm could you do?"

"Take me to bed and find out." He smirked and sat a few feet away on the grass, still holding the apple.

She shook her head and rolled her eyes. "It's a poison apple."

Tiberius looked at the apple's shiny black skin. "Who in their right mind would eat this?"

"It won't stay that way, you sodden-witted imp."

He cringed at the insult. "Well, who's it for?"

"As if I'd tell you."

He raised his sleeve and showed her a surprisingly muscular arm. "I'll throw it and you'll never find it. Some animal will eat it. And don't lie, I can spot a farce a mile away."

"Alright! It's for the queen. Happy?" She crossed her legs and folded her arms across her chest, then snorted out a breath and glared at him.

Tiberius stared at her, eyebrows raised. "That is horrible; I can't believe you told me." He blurted this out before he had a mind to consider his own safety, but the woman simply laughed. It made him relax, and as he studied her face, looking beyond her beauty, he realized he recognized her.

"You're Lady Sypheria, the queen's sister."

She raised an eyebrow and smirked. "You've heard of me?"

"Indeed. Well met, my lady. Should I stand and bow?"

"I think under the circumstances we can skip the formalities. Now, may I have my apple?"

Tiberius gripped the blackened fruit tighter. "Do you want any help?"

"What makes you think I need help?"

"Because if you were powerful enough, I'd be dead already, not sitting here holding your precious apple. You're not above needing aid."

"Not as dumb as you look, are you? I have already tried to kill her." She held up two fingers. "Twice."

"How?"

"The first time was with an enchanted comb. I used a glamour to change my appearance. Posed as a servant and snuck it into her chambers. It was another two weeks before she finally put it in her hair." She smiled and leaned forward. "It worked. She collapsed in a coma that no one could wake her from. I was weak from casting, so the king assumed we'd both been poisoned."

"Then what happened?" he asked, interested.

She scoffed and sat back, shaking her head. "True love's kiss."

"Oh." Tiberius frowned. "Why not hire someone to kill her?"

"I tried that. I engaged the services of a huntsman to bring me her heart and liver, which I later ate. Then I found out the queen still lived, and I had feasted on the internal organs of a deer." She screwed up her face to show how distasteful it all was.

"You were going to eat your sister's heart? That's disgusting."

"You have no idea how magic works, so don't judge me."

"Did you at least cook it?" Tiberius said, screwing up his nose. The way the witch glared at him told him it was time to drop the subject. "What happened to the hunter?"

"I hired someone else to kill him."

"So, why not have him kill Queen Ariella for you?"

She sighed. "Because when she fell pregnant with Snow White, she had a protection spell put on her. I couldn't kill her so easily."

"Snow White is around two and a half years old, is she not? So, you've been plotting this murder for a while."

"Yes." Her head sagged.

"So, the apple will…"

"Put the queen in another coma," she said.

"But won't true love's kiss just rouse her again?"

"Yes, that's why I have to get her out of the palace, hide her far from here."

Tiberius thought for a moment, then tossed the witch her apple. He slid his hand into his pocket, felt for the piece of glasz he always carried, and fingered its knobbly surface. He smiled. "I might be able to help."

# CHAPTER THREE

LATER THAT EVENING, after the dwarves had retired to their matching beds, Tiberius and the witch, Sypheria, stood in his work shed admiring the mountain of glasz. It gleamed, even in the dim light seeping through the cracks and tiny windows.

"We call it Glasz," Tiberius said. "But it's like no other gem we have found. I can't melt, cut, or break it. It's very strong. If you could somehow use your magic to make it workable, I might be able to make you something to help with your little problem."

Sypheria tapped her chin as she paced in front of the pile.

He stood and watched her pick up a gem and roll it in her hand. She tossed it in the air and caught it, closed her fingers around the hard rock, then spun to face the dwarf. "I may be able to cast a spell, make the glasz pliable."

"Assuming my magic works, how will that help me?"

Tiberius grinned. "I was thinking I could fashion some sort of a container, around six feet long and two feet wide. One that will be unbreakable."

"You mean a coffin." It wasn't a question.

Sypheria smiled and nodded. "How long would it take to complete?"

"I could get it done in a week," he said.

"And you'll want payment."

"Naturally. And a title."

"Ha! A title too."

"I will accept nothing less. This would solve your biggest problems, and I think that deserves a generous payment." Tiberius stood tall, unblinking.

"Indeed. When I become queen, I can bestow a title upon you and the land with it. Until then, you will be in my employ. You'll receive a generous wage and get lodgings in the castle. Close by, so you are at my beck and call." Sypheria smiled.

Tiberius didn't know if he could trust her, but a chance to live at the castle was too exciting an opportunity to pass up, so he agreed, and they shook hands.

"Good. Does anyone else you know of use the clearing? Your little friends, perhaps?" She waved her hand in the direction of the cabin.

Tiberius shook his head. "No, I've never seen anyone there. Except you."

"I need the moonlight. Bring all the glasz to the clearing tomorrow night; the moon will still be full enough. I'll perform a spell that'll help you manipulate the material any way you choose."

TIBERIUS TRIED to get a couple of hours of sleep, but he was restless, too excited from meeting the witch. He watched the moon through the small window by his bed as it moved unhurriedly across the night sky. When it looked at its highest and fullest, he crept out of bed and into his workshop.

Tiberius piled up the hand cart with the largest pieces of glasz, then placed the smaller shards into two large hessian sacks, which he threw on top of the cart. Next, he added his tools and, dragging the cart behind him, headed towards the forest. He grunted with the effort, his short but muscular legs doing most of the work. When he reached the thickest part of the forest, he swore and dropped the cart. The trees crowded together, and there was no way the cart was going to fit in between them. He would have to move the glasz the rest of the way to the clearing by hand. Tiberius slung the bags over each shoulder and trudged forward.

"What's taking so long?" Sypheria was sitting on his smoking stump.

"I can't get the cart through; it has to all be bought in by hand," he said as he dumped the bags in front of her. He headed back to his cart, then turned to see she hadn't moved. "Aren't you going to help me?"

She raised an eyebrow and smirked. "Don't be ridiculous. I need to work on my spell."

He left, mumbling under his breath about how it all better be worth it. He knew it would be. She had promised him gold, sure, and lots of it, but she had also promised him power. When she was queen, she would bestow upon him a lordship and land. He would finally have a home of his own and sleep in a bed fit for a king! The others could die in the mines for all he cared.

He was sweating profusely by the time he had gathered all of the glasz in a pile in the center of the clearing as well as his portable forge. Sypheria was standing near the heap casting, as he watched slumped against a tree, his eyelids fluttered closed.

BRIGHT LIGHT PERMEATED his closed lids; he sat up and stared at Sypheria, who was bathed in the moon's luminous light once again. Light enveloped her and the glasz in its glow. Time seemed to stop as he watched her cast the enchantment in a language he couldn't understand. As before, the column of light dissipated, blanketing the clearing in an ethereal glow, and Sypheria collapsed.

After seeing to her recovery, Tiberius started his work. The material now moved languidly in his grasp, almost as if it could read his thoughts. When he wished to cut a large piece, the saw barely needed to touch the glasz before it parted like water under the blade. If he wanted to fuse it, he brought the flame to it, and the ends would soften as he pressed the pieces together, then immediately harden. He continued his crafting well into the wee hours of the morning, hammering at the glasz and manipulating its shape to fit his plans.

Sypheria had prepared breakfast from supplies she had brought, a simple meal of oatcakes, hard cheese, and dried fruits, with a skin of goat's milk to wash it down.

Tiberius watched the sun's orange glow spread across the forest before eventually stretching through the clearing.

"You best get back to your dwarf companions. You'll need sleep too," Sypheria said, her gaze fixed on the rising sun.

He grunted and shrugged. "They'll be awake already. I'll tell them I went for a morning walk. I doubt they'd be suspicious." He nodded towards the forge and glasz. "What about all this?"

"I've been working on a cloaking spell. It should last until tonight when you return."

He nodded, broke off a piece of oatcake, and chewed. It was much sweeter and tastier than the oatcakes he normally ate.

"You'll have to get it done before the waning moon," she said. "The moon is at its most powerful whilst full; once it begins to wane, the spell will wear off, and the glasz will harden."

"But that's four days from now. I told you it would take a week," he spat. A few crumbs flew from his mouth and onto her dress.

She grimaced and wiped a delicate hand across the material. "I know, but it's all my magic can do."

He continued to eat as he watched her pack her things. He would have to get the job done if he had any hope of being paid and receiving the other rewards the witch promised. This was his bargaining chip. If he couldn't produce it in time, he would have nothing. He would be worth nothing to her.

# CHAPTER FOUR

For the next four days, Tiberius worked the glasz, and finally, on the fourth night, it was complete. Sypheria was to come to the clearing when the moon was at its highest, so the dwarf sat and ate the barley bread and salted fish he had brought, admiring his creation.

He had to admit, he had outdone himself. It was magnificent —a perfect, transparent coffin. The seams were decorated with intricately carved glasz, shaped in undulating waves. At the top of each corner was the figure of a woman, voluptuous and long-haired, gazing skyward. Inside were silken white sheets and a matching pillow. The witch might ask why he had spent such time on these details, but to Tiberius, everything he crafted was a work of art. Though no one aside from himself and Sypheria would know he had made it, doing his best was part of who he was: an artist.

He finished his meal and ruffled his beard, shaking loose the crumbs that had fallen. As he stood, he heard footsteps and glanced towards the trees.

Sypheria emerged like a dream; her shiny sky-blue dress

shimmered in the moonlight, its train moving fluidly across the ground behind her. She smiled when she reached him; then her eyes scanned the box. He beamed with pride at her reaction. Her jaw dropped as she ran her fingers over the smooth surface. He watched as her fingertips bounced along the waves until they reached one of the women. She stroked the upturned face of the figure and sighed.

"This is amazing. It seems almost a shame to use it for its designated purpose." She laughed. "But I still will."

Tiberius smiled. "So, what is the plan from here? How will you make her eat the apple? How will you get her in there?" He glanced at his masterpiece, then back at the witch who was smiling down at him.

Tiberius sat crouched behind a large oak, his gaze fixed on the road as he listened to the distant noise of carriage wheels approaching. Across the road lay a broken branch—too large to go around; the carriage would need to stop.

The sound of hoofbeats pounded the road, heralding their approach, a rhythmic drum beating like the refrain of an army marching to war. When it rounded the bend, he saw the four white horses first, their hooves kicking up dust as they moved in an easy gallop. When the carriage came into view, he sucked in a breath. The cab was a rich royal blue with large golden wheels and ornamental trim along the hubs and the top. The driver sat on a seat cushioned in royal blue velvet. On each corner of the cab were large lanterns, unlit but gleaming under the harsh rays of the sun. On the cabin door was the royal insignia, a crowned winged griffin; the king's ancestor laid claim to killing one of the great beasts. Four guards on horseback trotted on either side of the carriage.

He watched as the first two horses reared up and stopped, then heard men shout orders to each other. They suspected the trap, but the witch's henchmen were already attacking. The driver took an arrow to the chest, and Tiberius watched crimson bloom across the man's tunic before he toppled from the carriage.

Queen Ariella drew back a silk curtain and peered outside, her face pale, her eyes wide with alarm. The guards drew their swords, ready to confront their assailants and die for their queen. Arrows flew, piercing the flanks and chests of the Queen's Guard's horses. The men who weren't thrown from their mounts were pulled from them or slaughtered in their saddles.

The remaining guards cut down at least three of Sypheria's men. Swords clanged, men shouted, and a cold fear spread through the dwarf's veins. *Swing, parry, swing, parry.* It was a blur of bodies and blood. One of the witch's men lost an arm, cut through at the elbow. The appendage fell to the dirt and rolled a few paces. Hearing the man's screams of agony made Tiberius cringe. Another man thrust his sword through the neck of a guard, the blade protruding through the front. Tiberius felt the acidic taste of bile at the back of his throat.

Sypheria's men outnumbered the queen's guards. Dressed in black, their faces masked, they made a formidable and frightening sight as they cut down their enemies, their blades soaked with crimson sludge. The dwarf watched as the dirt road was painted with the blood of the fallen.

One of the men yanked open the carriage door, stabbed the guard inside, and pulled the screaming Ariella out by her arm. She fell in a puddle of blood, then scurried to her feet and ran towards the woods.

*Wrong way.* Tiberius shuffled as he watched and waited. It started to rain; the grey sky opened and poured a deluge over the scene; the water mixed with the blood, making everything wet and pink. Another black-clad man blocked the queen's path and pointed his sword at her. She turned and ran in the opposite direction. No one chased her. The slaughter continued as she ran towards the trees. Towards Tiberius.

# CHAPTER FIVE

Tiberius bolted to his allocated space, a mile away from the road, and casually started picking sprite berries. He swung a basket from his arm, already half-filled with berries he had picked earlier. When he heard the sound of footfalls behind him, he stopped and turned. He watched Queen Ariella shoving branches aside as she ran between trees. Her slim frame squeezed through the gaps, but both her dress and dark hair were sodden, and her crown was missing.

When she saw the dwarf, she changed her direction and headed for him, calling out in alarm.

"Please help me." She was breathing heavily, her ashen face a mask of fear. Her arms were bare from the elbow down and marked with faint red scratches from wayward branches. Several twigs had gotten caught in her hair, and she had the look of a panicked rabbit in her eyes. The front of her golden dress was splattered with her guard's blood which the rain was turning pink.

Tiberius dropped the basket and hurried towards her.

"What is it, milady?"

"Please, I'm in danger. My men were attacked. They're killing everyone!"

Pushing his sympathy aside, he nodded with a look of concern he hoped seemed genuine. "I live nearby; you can hide there. Come with me." He tugged on her hand and led her towards the cottage he shared with the other dwarves. As he passed, he kicked the basket of fruit aside, no longer needing it.

Once inside, Ariella hurriedly closed the curtains and paced up and down the small parlor. Tiberius handed her a towel to dry herself, boiled water, and made tea. He knew the other dwarves would be in the mine for several more hours, but he still felt a sense of urgency. He encouraged her to be seated and tell him what happened.

"I thank you for your help. I am Queen Ariella."

Tiberius bowed. "My apologies, Your Majesty, I didn't recognize you." He gestured towards her wet and bloody gown.

She waved him away and wiped her face with the towel. Unaware he had watched the attack, Queen Ariella explained she had been on a diplomatic mission, heading to Whitefall Kingdom on the other side of the mountains, when the ambush occurred. Her men were slaughtered, and she had run for her life.

He listened as she talked, reassuring her she was safe inside his modest home.

"You must be hungry," he stood. "I'm sorry, I dropped my basket of berries, and my cupboards are nearly bare. I do have this, though." The witch's apple sat in his palm. He curled his pudgy fingers around it, mesmerized by its perfection, and set it in the center of a small plate.

"It's alright, I'm not hungry."

He turned around and watched her eyes take in the sight of the apple, red and shiny. Its aroma sweetened the air, making his mouth water. He placed it in front of her. She licked her lips, and Tiberius smiled reassuringly. He needed her to take a bite.

"Please, you must eat something."

She nodded and smiled. "Perhaps you are right." She grabbed

the apple and took a big bite. The juice dripped down her chin as she slowly chewed and swallowed. She raised her hand to wipe it away, then dropped it back onto her lap as though the weight of it was too much.

"Mmm," she managed to say before her eyes fluttered closed, and she fell from the chair.

He rushed over to prevent her from smashing her head against the stone as the bitten apple rolled from her hand and across the floor. As he crouched beside the queen, the door burst open, and two of Sypheria's men entered, grabbed the woman, and carried her out of the cabin. Another man grabbed the apple and pocketed it. Outside, the men carried the queen into the forest, towards the glasz coffin.

Tiberius raced along behind them; their long strides meant he had to almost sprint to keep pace, but he soon fell behind. When he reached the clearing, he leant against a tree to catch his breath. Ariella was already inside the box, and the men were securing the lid in place.

Sypheria chanted, her hands weaving an intricate pattern in the air. Arcs of white light burst from her palms as she manipulated the elements of nature, creating a tapestry of color that swirled around her.

He staggered towards them, still out of breath from his run. One of the men frowned at him and stopped short of the group, not wanting his movement to distract her. She continued her casting, her eyes closed and hands in constant motion. They watched in silence, enchanted by the bursts of color trailing from her fingers as they danced, mesmerized by the melodic sound of her voice as she sang the strange but beautiful language.

"It's done," she finally said. Her hands dropped to her sides, and she swayed until one of her guards held her steady. The air stilled, and the colors faded away. "Brenton, fetch the mallet."

Sypheria's largest and most intimidating guard stepped towards the coffin, swung the heavy mallet over his shoulder, and bashed it against the top. The stone end bounced off and knocked Brenton off balance, making him stagger forward. Everybody leaned closer. There were gasps when they saw the glasz was unblemished. No scratch or dent marked its pristine surface. The witch clapped and laughed.

"Again," she said.

Brenton tried again, this time coming at a different angle.

Tiberius lost count of the times Brenton swung his mallet, but the man was sweating profusely when Sypheria called the next man to try. Each person had a different weapon or tactic. One tried to pry open the lid, but it wouldn't budge. Another doused the coffin in flames, but the fires seemed to slide off the glasz and onto the ground, where the men had to stamp it out. It was impenetrable. Sypheria strode over to Tiberius, knelt before him, and planted a kiss on his forehead.

"You're a genius. Come, we shall celebrate," she said as she headed away from the clearing.

He stepped towards the coffin and watched the queen's steady breathing.

"So, what will happen to her now? She'll suffocate?" he asked, feeling a twinge of guilt.

Sypheria paused. "Yes, I suppose. Either that or starve to death. Are you coming?"

Four of her men jostled past him and picked up the glasz prison. They headed in a different direction through the forest. Tiberius caught up with the witch and the remaining men.

"Where are they taking her?"

"They're going to drop her into the sea."

# CHAPTER SIX

Tiberius awoke with a hard bulge between his stocky legs and a smile adorning his sun-worn face. He stretched, yawned, and squashed his head further into the down-filled pillow. Reluctantly, he opened his eyes. It had been months since the attack, but a small part of him was convinced he would spoil the dream and discover he was once again sleeping in a single bed, surrounded by seven idiots.

He squinted before his eyes would open to take in the opulence that surrounded him. He wasn't looking at the dingy, dank ceiling of his old cottage but the luxurious green material that draped the four-poster bed in which he lay. He scanned the room, taking in the magnificence: the carved wooden panels, the tapestries, loveseat, and rugs all thick and warm, with the same forest green mixed in between more colors than he had seen in his life. In the corner was a tremendous fireplace, its marble mantle smooth and flawless, without a trace of dust.

"Son of a whore," he muttered.

"Mmm." The dark-haired woman beside him groaned and shifted in her sleep.

"Sypheria?" Tiberius frowned at the back of her head, then shifted onto an elbow and moved the hair from her face.

Not Sypheria. Not nearly as beautiful. He tried to think of who she was. His head pounded, an echo of the rum he had drunk the night before during a rowdy card game with a few of the witch's men. He wondered if Sypheria knew a spell to ease the ache in his head and churn in his belly.

Tiberius smiled as he took in the resplendent room, a reward for his aid in Sypheria's rescue. The story was complete folly, an excuse to invite the dwarf to court and deposit him in his quarters, only a wing away from the witch's section of the palace. He glanced at the woman beside him.

*Probably a whore.* Yes, he thought. That was it. They had drunkenly wandered into a brothel in town, but how the hell did he get her back here? Perhaps soon-to-be lords can do anything they want. He laughed, and the girl stirred. He sidled up behind her and pressed his manhood against her back.

"Wake up, my love. You have work to do."

"I can't make you a lord until I am queen."

Tiberius sat in Sypheria's parlor, eating dried fruits and syrup cake as he watched her pace. For a moment, he wondered if she had poisoned the food, fearing he knew too much. He was relieved when he didn't drop dead after the first few bites.

She turned and sloshed wine from her glass, the dark liquid spreading across the silver and gold rug—a stain her chambermaid would probably be blamed for.

"You should have seen the performance I put on about how you helped save my life from those bandits just to get you in here. You should be thanking me!"

"I did thank you, but I thought we were a team. How many times do you want to hear it?"

She glared at him. "I just want to know that you appreciate the groveling I did on your behalf. I could have left you at that stinking cabin."

Tiberius frowned at her, but it didn't sound like a serious threat. He watched as she resumed her pacing. Sypheria's room was much more extravagant than his own and much larger, which is why most meetings they had were held there. He sat at the table in the salon, just off her bedchamber. The fabric that covered the cushioned chairs was pink and silver; the wooden table painted white mixed with tendrils of gold that spread across the surface like ripples on a pond.

He refilled his chalice with rich red wine and offered to refill hers. She held her glass out to him, and he filled it almost to the brim, then stifled a chuckle when she plonked herself down on the pink and gold loveseat, spilling wine on her dress.

"Auroch's balls!" She wiped her dress and took a long gulp from her glass.

"I appreciate what you did. If you want me to show you how much, why don't you come and sit on my face?" He waggled his tongue at her.

"You're a disgusting pig," she spat.

"It might help you relax. Why are you so stressed?"

Now she glared at him, her eyes narrowed, and for once, Tiberius was nervous.

"Don't you know?"

He shrugged. "Know what?"

"If you thought about more than your dick for five minutes, you'd have heard."

"Heard what?"

"The coffin. They found the accursed coffin!"

# CHAPTER SEVEN

THE COFFIN HADN'T SUNK as Sypheria's men assumed. The airtight seal had made the glass buoyant, so they weighed it down with large rocks, securing them with rope until, eventually, it disappeared under the water. They went back and proclaimed their success with no mention of the difficulties they had had.

The sea, unhappy with this morbid gift, had surged forward, the waves pushing against the boulders and loosening the ropes that had held the casket in place. After a few days, the box was free to roll with the undertow, moving closer to the shore with each wave. Eventually, it was beached, not far from the dwarves' cottage.

Seven little men had been conducting a search, not for the missing queen, but for their fellow dwarf, Tiberius, who seemed to have also disappeared, when they came upon the coffin, resting askew against a boulder.

~

TIBERIUS WATCHED FROM HIS WINDOW, which looked out onto the town square where they had placed the coffin after the king's men had failed to open it. The king stood on the podium, Sypheria to his left, and two men Tiberius didn't know to his right. From his window, he could make out most of the speech. He had stayed out of sight since hearing the coffin had been found by the other dwarves, or *'Your stupid little friends,'* as Sypheria put it. They would have no idea he was there and no reason to think he had been living in the palace. He trusted they were clueless enough not to realize it was made of glasz.

Tiberius had replaced the missing glasz with piles of rocks and covered them with blankets. He doubted they had checked his workshop other than a cursory glance to see if he was inside. However, if they saw him there, the leap to what had happened wouldn't be too hard to make, so he thought it wise to remain hidden until the other dwarves were out of the city. He might have some of Sypheria's men pay the dwarves a visit, in case they had noticed the missing gems or started to question the coffin's origins. There's nothing like the threat of broken bones to seal the lips of the meek.

"People of Woodhaven," the king began, "I have brought my queen, *our* queen, here for an important reason. The palace healer says she's alive and under a spell. He believes that if we can open this coffin soon, he may be able to reverse the spell. Ariella's sister and I," he waved a hand towards Sypheria, who bowed her head, "are not ready to mourn yet. We have hope and faith that someone out there can help us. Anyone who can open this coffin, by any means, without causing undue harm to my wife, will be richly rewarded." He paused to wipe his eyes with the back of his hand. "I would be forever grateful, and your reward would be beyond your wildest dreams. I implore you for aid."

He stepped off the podium, and people began to slowly approach the sleeping queen. A few men rapped their knuckles against the top, unsure of how aggressive to be. After the king, Sypheria, and his advisors were out of sight, the men cast glances towards the guards left behind.

"Go ahead," one of them said. "We've tried everything."

This egged the men on, and they attacked the coffin with all their strength. Over the course of the next few hours, men came and went, arriving with various tools.

Tiberius watched to see if they came up with anything new Sypheria's men hadn't already tried. By nightfall, they had brought their torches. The dwarf watched the warm glow from the comfort of his room and smiled to himself about what a genius he was.

"YOU PUT on quite a performance up there. I almost believed you were truly grief-stricken, standing on the dais beside the king." Tiberius took a swig of ale as he reclined on Sypheria's soft divan.

She raised an eyebrow and smirked. "Really? Perhaps I should join the mummers."

"I think the audience will be too enamored by your beauty and too busy staring at your tits to hear anything you say."

She smiled, leaned forward, and tapped him on the nose with her index finger. "You amuse me. That's the only reason I keep you around."

"Anyone suspect me of making the coffin?"

"No, I've taken care of that. I've sent my men to question local cabinet makers and gem merchants."

"Really?" Tiberius furrowed his brow.

"Don't worry. I trust my men. They've been sent to spend a few days visiting alehouses and brothels. They'll report back to the king of how they asked around and found out nothing."

He could tell she was drunk. She always had a few drinks before one of the king's banquets, her way of preparing for what she found to be a tedious evening of fake airs. Tiberius was enjoying the expensive ale and the view of her milky white skin busting out the top of her bodice.

She sat back and took another gulp of her wine. He watched her smooth neck as she tilted her head. She lowered the glass, saw him staring, and smirked.

"You know, I'm never going to sleep with you."

"Never say never, witch. One day you'll drink too much, and I'll have my way with you." He could only get away with calling her that when she was drunk, and he relished the opportunity to feel like he had a little power, even if it was an illusion.

She stood and swayed. Tiberius leapt to his feet and grabbed her elbow to steady her.

"Ha, ha! I'll never be that drunk," she said as she walked to her dresser.

He laughed. She was plenty drunk, but would he take advantage of her that way? *What kind of man would that make me?* He pushed the thought aside, knowing it was probably best not to sleep with her anyway. She would likely kill him the next morning.

"So, why all the hatred for Ariella? What did she do?"

Sypheria spun around to glare at him. "That bitch stole everything from me."

*Porgus's Balls, she really is drunk.* Tiberius tried to look sympathetic, knowing any information he could get might put him in a better position.

She stumbled back to her seat across from the dwarf and sloshed more wine into her glass.

"I was supposed to marry Cedric. It was me who should've been queen."

"What happened?"

She let out a huff of breath. "I was the elder and the most beautiful, and it was arranged that I would be wed to Cedric. My parents sent me to the Kingdom of Valence to learn more about matters of court and diplomacy so I could speak with the king and widen my knowledge and circle of influence. It was such a good plan, but by the time I'd gotten back, the cur had fallen in love with my sister!"

Tiberius didn't have a chance to speak before she started ranting again.

"Ariella didn't want me to be jealous, oh no. 'Come and live in the palace with me,' she said. Like that was going to make up for it. Then, two years later, Snow White was born. The curd in the cream puff!" A sneer spread across her face, and she threw her wine glass into the hearth. It shattered, the pieces twinkling as they caught the light. "Ariella was living my life! All of it!" She stood and bumped her thigh against the table. "Horse shit."

He could see she was close to tears. He stood and offered her his arm, but she waved it away. "I don't need you; I don't need anyone."

"Of course not," he said.

"I'm a powerful witch, you know. I could crush them all."

"I know, but that's not the right way and you know it. You still need loyal subjects to rule over."

She stumbled towards her bed and flopped onto it in the most ungracious way. Tiberius felt a stirring in his loins at her vulnerability but turned away.

"I'm not going; tell the king I'm sick."

"But it's the child's birthday. Your absence will seem strange."

"I don't care."

"It'll be suspicious." He waited as she sat up.

"Very well. I'll go, but I'm going to hate every second of it."

"That's all right. People will think you're grieving for your sister."

He held out his hand, which she took, and he pulled her up off the bed. She wobbled a few steps and laughed.

"We need to sober you up."

"It's fine." She moved to her dresser and removed a small vial. She spoke an incantation and poured the contents into her cup. A wisp of purple smoke swirled around the inside of the glass, then settled back into the liquid. She gulped it down, and when she turned, she smiled. Her eyes looked clearer, her face no longer flushed, and she walked straight and true.

"That's incredible," said Tiberius.

"It's a glamour spell. Very handy." She winked and headed for the door.

# CHAPTER EIGHT

Unlike Sypheria, Tiberius loved a party, and this was the first banquet he had attended. While she sulked on the dais next to the king and the princess, he sat in the middle of one of the long tables that ran the length of the hall in awe of the opulence and extravagance. He had struggled to keep his eyes from betraying his lack of sophistication when he was first seated.

The table was covered with platters of food; the aromas floated towards his nostrils like angels carrying whispered dreams, making his mouth water. There were loaves of bread with crusts so golden, they made a hollow drum beat when hit with the end of a knife, and roast duck with crispy skin that dripped juices into the vegetables that surrounded it at the bottom of the dish. Towards each end of the table sat grilled salmon, savory tarts, and plates piled high with meat-filled parcels; the flaky pastry crumbled whenever the table was jostled. In the middle of the table sat a whole suckling pig, flanked by two herb-crusted pheasants and several bowls of thick stew and baked potatoes. The pig's skin gleamed in the candlelight, and Tiberius's eyes were drawn to the rosy apple stashed between its jaws. His thoughts flashed briefly to the apple that had inadvertently brought him to the palace.

He wanted to taste it all, so he drank and ate everything that was put in front of him until he was ready to burst. He was full after his second helping of the roast pheasant and jelly, and still, there was food in front of him, so he would pick at what was there. The food was such a contrast to the fare he had shared with the other dwarves: bland stews, hard bread, and tough meat.

He was thoroughly enjoying himself; he flirted with the women at the table around him, despite the fact that many were with their husbands. He would pinch the bottom of every serving girl who refilled his spiced wine and sing loudly with other drunkards when the bard played songs he was familiar with.

The table was cleared and then, to Tiberius's amazement, restocked with a variety of other foods—platters of fresh fruit: sugar melons, apples, plump raisins, and faeberries. Cheeses and thinly sliced meats, boiled eggs, meatballs with ginger and honey glaze, and scones served with an assortment of spiced jellies. He wondered how he would fit any more food into his belly, but somehow, he managed.

Before dessert was served, the bards took a break, and the entertainment became comical with jugglers, jesters, and a puppet show. They did their best to impress the princess, both with their skills and their comedic timing. The jugglers pretended to lose track of juggling balls only to catch them in their hats. The jesters tumbled around the hall in their colorful checkered attire and brought cheers and laughter from the crowd. The puppet show was the most humorous of the acts, Tiberius thought. The mock stage was set up with two hideously ugly wooden dolls, and rather than the fairytale story he had expected, it was a tale of an unusually aggressive husband and wife who constantly got on each other's nerves. No doubt Snow White enjoyed it for the lavishly dressed and boisterous behavior of the marionettes, but the show was for the adults and every married couple in the room nodded along and laughed know-ingly. Tiberius was thankful he wasn't shackled to a nagging wife.

The meal was finished with dessert, a delectable display of marzipan cakes, sweet tarts, candied fruit, sugared almonds, and cream puffs filled with lemon curd. As he wiped the crumbs of his last tart from his beard, there was a tug at his tunic. He looked down into the deep blue eyes of the birthday girl. Her raven hair was as dark and silky as ink, her porcelain skin flawless as any child's. Her rosy cheeks turned more crimson as she cleared her throat to speak.

"Excuse me, I'm a princess. I'm three today and I'd like to dance."

Tiberius chuckled and glanced at the dance floor where couples began to pair off, forming two lines and facing each other as the music played. He was not much of a dancer. In fact, he struggled to think of a time when he had ever danced with a woman. Though Snow White was just a child, he looked back into her hopeful eyes and found he couldn't refuse her. He stood and bowed.

"I'd be honored, my lady." He grabbed her hand and led her to the dance floor. He was only a foot taller than her and suspected that was why she had asked him to dance—she wanted to feel like a grown-up. He followed her lead, moved forward as she did, and clapped his hands or kicked his feet when the men around him did. When he linked arms with her and whirled her about, she would giggle.

He saw Sypheria smirk every time he spun the child around and hoped the whole room wasn't laughing at him. It was not like he could've said no.

# CHAPTER NINE

No one had been able to break open the coffin. The king had sent for every magician, conjuror, enchantress, and wizard from every neighboring kingdom, but they, too, failed to open it and free the queen.

In desperation, the king sought out a dark sorcerer, one known to dabble in only the crudest magic, the man feared by all good men: Daramond the Displacer. Legend said he could transport people and objects to other realms. His hope was that the evil man could remove Ariella from her magical prison before it was too late. Against the advice of his council, the heartbroken king called for his aid and promised the sorcerer land and power if he could bring back his queen.

~

"When is he due to arrive?" Sypheria wrung her hands. Tiberius had never seen her so anxious.

"In one week," Gradian, her guard commander, replied.

"What's the concern? No one can open it nor break it, and there's no sorcerer more powerful than you. You said so your-

36

self," Tiberius said.

"If there is anyone that can ruin my plan to get on the throne, it'll be him. We must stop him."

She looked at her guard. "Take as many men as you can without looking suspicious, dress in the king's guards' colors, and meet him on the road. Tell him King Cedric has sent an escort, then *escort* him along a dark, lonely path, and when the opportunity strikes, kill him."

"Yes, my lady."

"And bring me his heart!"

The man left, and Tiberius shook his head.

"*What?*" she snapped.

"You worry too much. Have you seen the queen?"

"No."

"It's been months; your apple enchantment is wearing off. Her skin is grey and hanging from her bones. She's starving. Once the magic has faded, won't she simply die?"

"Yes, I think so, but I can't take any chances. And what if this Daramond can cast a spell and magic her out of the coffin?"

"Then it was all for naught."

Eight of Sypheria's men were sent to deal with Daramond. Eight skilled swordsmen who thought they could surprise the mage and kill him before he reached the outskirts of the kingdom. Only one man remained. He staggered into Sypheria's room, looking pale and sickly.

"Is he dead?" said Sypheria. The guard shook his head.

"What happened?" Tiberius asked.

"It was awful. Blood everywhere. Two men were impaled by branches, another two had their throats slit by their own swords."

"What? How?" said Tiberius.

"Daramond just waved his hands around and chanted something, and men were thrown into trees and swords were ripped out of hands. He magically threw a boulder and smashed the side of Petrik's head. Half his face was gone!"

"What of the others?" said Tiberius.

"He pulled Bardol's heart from his chest without even touching him! He sucked the breath from my lungs just with a look."

"Then how did you escape?" asked Sypheria.

"He let me go. I think he wanted you to know we failed and how powerful he was."

"What of the last two men?" said Tiberius.

"I don't know. I think he broke their bones or something because they both collapsed and began screaming in pain. I've never heard such screams."

Sypheria stood and moved to the table. She poured herself a wine. Tiberius could see her hand shaking slightly. "You are dismissed."

The guard seemed surprised. "Thank you, my lady." He left quickly, and Tiberius turned to Sypheria.

"I think he thought you would kill him."

"I thought about it, but it appears as though I've lost seven good swordsmen. I need all the men I can get."

A few days later, there was a celebration as Daramond the Displacer arrived in the kingdom. Another banquet was organized for later in the week to honor the mage. He was put up in the king's most lavish guest rooms, and every whim or demand was met with enthusiasm by the servants. Everybody believed this man would save their queen. And perhaps he would, but not before he got what he wanted. That's the way of certain people.

Tiberius sat on Sypheria's window ledge on the west side of the castle and watched the dark mage wander the gardens.

Despite the warmth of the sun, the man still wore his long black cloak. He was surprised to see Daramond was not the wrinkled old codger he had imagined. He was, in fact, middle-aged, distinguished, and handsome. His dark brown hair had the slightest sprinkling of salt and pepper, which only made him look wiser.

Sypheria leaned out of the window to take a peek at the man who was causing her such grief.

"Do you think he suspects you of trying to kill him?"

Sypheria sighed. "No, there's no way he could know it was me. Besides, my men were wearing the kingdom's colors, so he'll assume it's someone from the palace."

"So, what will you do now?"

"I guess I'll have to kill Daramond myself."

"And how are you going to do that?"

"I haven't figured it out yet, but I will."

"You might not even have to. He's not here for altruistic reasons. He may just bleed the kingdom dry and not attempt to get her out at all," said Tiberius.

"With that kind of magic, what use has he for our coin? I expect he could get gold anytime."

Tiberius shrugged. "Maybe he does it for fun."

"Well, that's not the solution I want. When I take over as queen, I want there to be full coffers and no loose ends."

Tiberius shivered.

She smirked at him. "Not you. I still have uses for you."

The mage turned to face the window, and Sypheria smiled and waved. He narrowed his eyes at her, then offered a wave back.

"Can he tell you're a witch?" As far as Tiberius knew, only himself and her men were aware of it.

"I can sense his magic when he's near, so I'd imagine."

Before Daramond rounded the corner, he glanced back at the window. Sypheria tossed her hair and licked her lips. Though

Daramond tried to hide it, Tiberius saw the corner of the sorcerer's lip curl up in a smile before he was gone.

"I think I might have a way to get close to him after all..."

Tiberius chuckled. "Can I watch?"

~

TIBERIUS STOOD beside the queen's coffin and stared at Sypheria's window. He could make out their silhouettes behind the gauze curtains and imagined what was happening. He had watched as the witch gushed over the sorcerer during the welcome banquet; she marveled at his ability and used her womanly wiles to seduce him.

Tiberius wondered if sleeping with the sorcerer was part of Sypheria's plan. *Probably needs a spell to make him more potent.* He scoffed and drummed the top of the glasz with his fingers, which invited a few scowls from nearby guards and townsfolk who were holding a vigil. Drawing his hand away, he turned towards the palace. He wanted to know what the witch was going to do, curious to see how she would outsmart a mage more powerful than herself.

~

SNEAKING into her chambers proved more difficult than he had expected. If there was a secret passage inside, he was unable to find it. He sauntered to the door instead, emanating confidence only a man of his stature could exude.

"Whoa there. Where do you think you're going?"

"Step aside, Erwin, she's expecting me."

The guard leaned down towards Tiberius and lowered his voice. "No, she isn't, little man, she's entertaining a guest."

"I know, I'm here to help with the ... extermination."

Erwin and the other guard chuckled. "I don't think so. Move along. We know the plan, and you, my friend, are not part of it."

"Get going before you feel my boot up your behind," the other guard added.

"Hedge-born churls," Tiberius muttered under his breath as he walked away.

*Now what?* He wanted to get in there, wanted to know how she would kill a powerful warlock. But how?

*Boom*

Tiberius spun on his heel and hurried back to Sypheria's wing. The door was open, the guards already inside. Two more of her men rushed past the dwarf. He followed them through the parlor and into her bedchamber. He skidded to a stop and then cowered beside the dresser. Two men lay twisted and broken on the rug, dead. The witch stood on the opposite side of the bed from Daramond, her hands up as she chanted. The air shimmered around her, like heatwaves above a roaring campfire.

Tiberius snapped his hands over his ears as a second *boom* rang out, the result of the warlock trying to break through Sypheria's barrier of protection. She looked scared; her eyes were wide, and tears streaked her pallid face. Her hands trembled with concentration and effort. He wondered how long her shield could last against the onslaught of dark magic.

Inky shadows clung to the walls like fetid moss and blackened spores sprouted across the ceiling as Daramond's arcane magic spread through the room like a sentient beast. The air was soaked with the smell of dirt and rotting leaves, reminding Tiberius of a graveyard. *Decay.*

Another guard rushed the mage, and at Daramond's command, the man was knocked against the wall. The remaining guard slashed at the mage with his sword and managed to nick his arm. Tiberius watched in horrified awe as Daramond knocked the sword from his hand and towered over him, reciting an incantation. The air in the room surged. A maelstrom swirled around the dark mage as his words became louder and more menacing. The atmosphere became thick and heavy. Tiberius found it hard to breathe.

The cowering man abruptly disappeared, reappearing outside the window before plummeting to his death. His screams made Tiberius's balls shrivel. It seemed possible this sorcerer would be able to free Ariella from her cage if he wished.

He looked at Sypheria, whose eyes widened in fear. She mouthed, '*Help me*,' and he searched the room for something. Still hiding beside the dresser, the warlock hadn't seen him yet, and for once, the dwarf was thankful for his inconsiderable height. The guard who had been flung against the wall wasn't dead and emitted a low groan as he struggled to get up. Distracted by the guard, the warlock turned, and Tiberius seized the opportunity. He dashed forward, grabbed the discarded sword, and plunged it into the man's back in an upward direction, then dropped and rolled under the witch's bed. By the time the mage had swung around, Tiberius was out of sight and had crawled behind Sypheria and her protective bubble.

The injured guard managed to stand. He staggered forward and swung his arm. His sword carved an arc through the air as Daramond turned. The blade sliced a thick line across the mage's neck, then the guard collapsed.

Tiberius peered out from behind Sypheria's skirt and saw the warlock's hands clasp his neck, trying to hold the wound closed, his face a mask of shock. Blood oozed from between his fingers and across his hands; the crimson waterfall stained his dark robe as the man fell to his knees. His gaze lingered on the witch before he fell forward, his face slack and pale, his arms splayed. Blood pumped out in a few strong spurts, then slowed as the man's heart stopped. Sypheria dropped her hands and collapsed to the floor.

# CHAPTER TEN

With all the excitement around the death of Daramond the Displacer, no one from the palace had noticed that the witch's spell had finally worn off. It was a peasant named Grabor, who had travelled for days to pay his respects to the queen, who noticed her chest rise and fall and saw her eyelids flutter open.

"She's awake! She's alive!" He had shouted as he ran towards the palace guards who manned the main gate. "The queen has awoken!"

One guard rushed to the coffin to see if the man spoke the truth. When it was confirmed, a second guard ran to the palace to alert the king. A small crowd had gathered around her and tried desperately to pry off the lid with their hands, even though they all knew every man for miles had attempted to do so already. The queen's eyes were filled with raw terror as her fists banged weakly against the inside of the glass.

The king arrived, sank to his knees in front of the coffin, and wept, his hands pressed against the glasz. Queen Ariella flattened her palm against it, too, and mouthed words no one could hear or understand.

The people of Woodhaven Kingdom sat around their queen—

a hopeless vigil as they watched her die. After three hours, her eyes had closed again, and she took her last breath. The people wept and sang songs of mourning. The whole town was there, with the exception of Sypheria, who was still under the healer's orders for strict bed rest. Tiberius watched it all, then slipped away to tell the witch the good news.

# CHAPTER ELEVEN

"YOU MUST MOVE ON, sire. The contents of the coffin are no longer your beloved wife," said Rolamere, the head of the king's council and, unbeknownst to the king, another player in Sypheria's game. Tiberius wasn't fond of Rolamere. He was arrogant, and not only was he in the witch's pocket, but Tiberius suspected he had spent some time in her bed too. That bothered him, though he wasn't sure why; it's not like he had ever been there. Rolamere was only out for what he could get for himself. Tiberius frowned; wasn't he after the same?

After Daramond's death, Sypheria had convinced the king to let Tiberius join the council, explained how he had, yet again, helped save her life. Of course, the first time was a mummer's farce, this time was true. He deserved some recognition and reward. The king had argued that a seat on the council was far too big a leap for one such as Tiberius, but the affection he felt for his sister-in-law made him easy to manipulate, and he eventually relented.

The position was more for Sypheria than himself. She wanted another pawn on the council to do her bidding. He, however, was not one to complain. The position granted him power, a title, and coin. He scratched his bald chin; the witch had made him shave off his russet beard. *'You're not a blacksmith anymore; you need to look worthy of your position,'* she had told him. His clean-shaven face, neatly trimmed hair, and dapper outfit made him look the part, and he supposed he would get used to it. However, he felt as though it made him look like a young boy, but one didn't argue with Sypheria. It was a pointless and somewhat dangerous exercise. Though not as powerful as the dark mage Daramond had been, he saw the magic she wielded and wasn't about to get on her bad side.

"We need to remove the casket. The city has mourned long enough. You have mourned long enough," Rolamere said as the other council members nodded along.

"Sire," Tiberius said, "she requires a proper burial. You haven't been down there for a few days. Her beauty fades. It's unwise to allow the people to see that."

The king nodded but remained silent as he stared into the distance. No one spoke, allowing him a moment to take in what they were suggesting.

Tiberius had been down there that very morning, and the queen was rotting. The airtight seal had caused a strange decomposition. When she was still under Sypheria's spell, her body remained suspended halfway between life and death, but once the spell had worn off and the queen died, her body began to die, too.

Tiberius saying her beauty was fading was to spare the king the horrible truth. Her skin had gone from pale to a strange green, and her abdomen began to swell. Her skin blistered, he suspected from the sun, despite the shades the palace workers had erected. Her fingertips had begun to blacken, the fetid color spreading up her fingers like spilled ink. Her insides had started to liquify; the putrid contents leaked out of her nose, eyes, and mouth. Tiberius imagined what the smell would be like if the gases weren't trapped inside the coffin with her. He suspected if they didn't remove her soon, her skin would slough away completely, and they'd be looking at the skeleton of their former queen.

"With your permission, we'll organize a royal funeral," said a balding man Tiberius couldn't name.

The king nodded, then stood to leave.

"Ah, Sire," Rolamere said. "Forgive me, but since we have all gathered, there's another matter we should discuss. A rather sensitive one."

"More sensitive than discussing my wife's rotting body?" the king snapped. Every man around the table sucked in a breath; a few leaned back. The king, however, sat and gestured for Rolamere to continue.

"I think it's time to discuss when you plan to remarry."

"Remarry! My wife's not even buried," the king said.

"All due respect and sympathies, sire, but the queen should have been buried months ago. It's cruel to yourself and your people to have let her linger in that box for all to see," Rolamere said.

Tiberius swallowed and wondered if Rolamere knew what he was doing.

Rather than strike him, the king buried his head in his hands and sobbed quietly. No one spoke. No one seemed to even breathe. When the man had composed himself, he scanned the faces at the table. "Do you all agree?"

Most of the men nodded.

"Nothing brings the people more joy than a wedding. I realize the sensitive nature of the timing, but it'll be good to show the people that you are moving on and that the kingdom will have a queen again," Tiberius said.

"And the young princess needs a mother," a thin man named Claude said.

The king nodded, then turned to Rolamere. "Did you have someone in mind?"

*This is it.* Tiberius's stomach did a flip while he waited for Rolamere to answer.

"Might I suggest the Lady Sypheria? She is well respected, beautiful, and still young enough to produce an heir."

The king swallowed, no doubt remembering their history.

"You were supposed to be wed to her originally, were you not? The purpose for the alliance with Whitefall Kingdom. What better way to solidify the treaty?" said Rolamere. "Whitefall grieves for Ariella, too. She was our queen but still their daughter."

"Indeed. I suppose you are right. It's just..." The king paused. "Make the arrangements, assuming the Lady Sypheria has no objections."

"Of course, Sire."

The king adjourned the meeting and took his leave. One by one, the other members followed.

"Masterfully done," Tiberius said to Rolamere as they walked out.

"Thank you, and I appreciate your assistance." He gave the dwarf a nod. "Perhaps we should have a quiet celebration in honor of our soon-to-be queen. Tell me, Tiberius, do you have a penchant for brothels?"

The dwarf chuckled. "I do."

"Wonderful. I think we are going to get along splendidly."

# CHAPTER TWELVE

SYPHERIA'S DRESS was a silken-applique wonder. Ivory with gold and black embroidery, the intricate pattern covered the front of the bodice and ran down the three-quarter length sleeves, ending in delicate swirls at the cuff. The same design undulated down the ivory waves of the dress, culminating at the hem, then ran along the edge of the train that followed behind at least four dwarf lengths. It looked heavy and cumbersome. Off the shoulder with a cinched waist that forced her bosom upwards, the dress sparkled as she moved, the light of a hundred sconces reflected in the glasz beads she had had the seamstresses sew into the gown.

Ivory silk ribbons flecked with more glasz were woven into her long dark braid. And she wore a white-gold circlet upon her head, adorned with five-pointed oblong-shaped shards of glasz, carved by Tiberius himself. It made her shine like a mythical goddess.

He was less interested in the immaculate design of the dress and more about the large skirt, imagining what he could be doing if he was hiding underneath. His mind drifted along, tuning out the cleric as he performed the ceremony. Tiberius scanned the inside of the chapel. Garlands of purple and white frost flowers, held together with ivory ribbons, hung merrily on the walls, contrasting the stark white of the stonework. Windows dominated the front of the room, stretched gracefully from floor to ceiling into pointed arches, the glasswork a myriad of colorful panes, depicting various historical events.

The ruckus of clapping and cheers startled him from his daydreams, and he stood and clapped along, getting small glimpses of the bride and groom between the sweating bodies of the other guests. He squeezed through a gap and saw the couple walk past, hand in hand. Sypheria noticed him and winked before leaving the palace chapel with her new husband. The guests also left and headed to the ballroom for the grand feast.

More frost flowers were strewn across the floor, and as the guests entered their feet crushed the petals and released a pleasant fragrance into the air. Candles burned in chandeliers and gave the room a romantic, warm glow.

He stood in the queue and waited for his turn to present the king and soon-to-be queen with their wedding gift. He listened to the sounds of the gnarled wooden chair legs scraping the stone floor as guests took to their allocated seats. When he finally reached the front, his eyes scanned the pile of gifts that sat at the couple's feet. It was mostly small, intricately carved pieces of furniture, jewelry, and gold-plated everything. The lid of a box sat askew, and inside, he saw a set of four pewter chalices decorated with the royal insignia and symbol of a crowned winged griffin. Even those were no match for Tiberius's gift. He had spent weeks working on it and used up the last of the glasz they had, aside from what Sypheria had used for her dress and tiara. He had asked the witch to cast her enchantment on it so he could manipulate it without her knowing what he was crafting.

Now, though subtle, he could see her excitement. She sat straighter when he approached the dais; her eyes sparkled like a child with a full plate of sugar cookies. He stepped forward and offered a flourished bow.

"Your Majesty, my Queen, please allow me to present this humble gift in honor of your nuptials." He gestured for the huge man behind him to step forward. He carried a large item covered in purple cloth; it spanned from his shoulders to his knees when he held it abreast. He placed it on the floor next to the dwarf. Tiberius pinched the top of the cloth between his fingers and pulled it away.

There were audible gasps from Sypheria and from those close by who could see what it was.

"An exquisite gift, thank you, Tiberius," the king said.

"It's magnificent," Sypheria said as she placed her fingertips upon the top edge.

"There's no need to be gentle, my lady. It's quite strong," he whispered, and the witch suppressed a giggle.

To hide the fact the mirror was made of the same material as the coffin, he had tinted it with silver dye, so it wasn't quite clear but rather shimmered as the sterling flowed through the inside of the glasz like thin molten streams. He had made the pigment by mixing the silver berries of the sprite berry tree with candle wax. The designs were more delicate than any he had used before, more intricate; he doubted anyone would suspect the mirror and coffin were crafted by the same hand.

The mirror was oval. The reflective surface shined like a still pool in the moonlight. Tiberius had folded and shaped the glasz around the mirror to represent the branches of a tree; they spiraled in on one another like serpents, their crystalline leaves decorated the branches in perfectly placed clusters. He had even hand-carved each leaf, including the network of veins. At the top of the mirror sat a symmetrical glasz apple.

Sypheria withdrew her hand and bent low to kiss the dwarf's cheek.

"I love it."

# CHAPTER THIRTEEN

AFTER LIVING at court for so long, Tiberius had started to find the parties tedious. Since it had only been a month since the wedding, he would have much rather missed this banquet in favor of a drunken night of cards and whores, but it was expected of him to attend. He was in line for a lordship and, thus, had to behave in the manner befitting a person of great import. His excessive drinking and whoring were now done in secret, which didn't bother him too much, but dressing like a dandy and having to engage in polite conversation with a bunch of stuck-up nobles was work. On top of that, all they did was gossip about each other in the name of garnering favor from the king. He supposed he would have been no different had he not been in league with the witch. His time would come.

Most of the gatherings were for King Cedric to show off his wealth and the apple of his eye, Snow White. Sypheria played the part of doting stepmother and wife and only let the mask slip in the privacy of her chambers.

Tiberius made his way to the grand hall and took his usual seat. A serving girl ducked in between other guests to get to his table and fill his tankard of ale. He nodded and smiled.

"You know me well."

"Yes, my lord," she said. She dipped her head and scurried off like a frightened mouse.

The dwarf enjoyed his mead and watched as the new queen walked to the dais. The coronation was held earlier that day in the palace chapel. It was more tedious than the wedding. He was glad when it was over, and the guests were ushered to the hall for the banquet that followed. The party would go well into the night, but he would need to pace himself. Sypheria was queen now, but she still needed the king to grant the lordship.

The food was even more extravagant than at Snow White's birthday banquet, with an additional three courses, however, no way near as excessive as the wedding feast. Having learned what to expect, Tiberius was more selective of what he ate, never taking more than one helping of a dish, knowing there would be much more food to come. The entertainment was much the same, with the exclusion of a puppet show and the addition of a knife-throwing act and a mummer's play.

"Hello, Uncle 'Berius," Snow White said, her red lips stretched in a huge smile.

"Hello, Snow, how are you enjoying the party?"

"Oh, it's lovely. But nanny says I've got to go to bed now." Her smile vanished, and she looked longingly at the dance floor.

Tiberius glanced across the room to where the girl's nanny, Elia, was waiting. He had expected someone older, not the attractive young woman who stood near the doorway. The woman's dark blonde hair was tied in a bun, and she stood with her arms crossed. When she noticed him looking, she smiled but made a sleeping gesture with her hands.

"Well, nanny is right. It's late for young princesses to be dancing."

She threw her arms around his shoulders and kissed him on the cheek. He squeezed her in his arms, then released her.

She curtseyed. "Goodnight, Uncle 'Berius."

"Goodnight, Princess." He stood to bow in return.

The king's daughter scurried off towards where her nanny waited, and Tiberius turned to his drink. He glanced at the dais and saw the witch smiling at him, so he raised his glass to her. She did the same, and they both drank.

Snow had taken a liking to the dwarf, occasionally commenting on how he wasn't much taller than she, until some stuffy lord pointed out that was a rude thing to say. Tiberius hadn't minded and would often reply that she would tower over him one day.

The child took to following him around court and sometimes mimicked his actions. If he took some grapes, she would do the same. If he put his arms behind his back, Snow would put her arms behind her back as well. Her impressions were uncanny, regardless of their marked difference in age and beauty. Tiberius found her to be much less annoying than he had imagined. She was quiet and polite, trained to behave as a princess, not a rowdy child. He had noticed she wouldn't imitate his less redeeming actions, such as belching after a meal, though he tried to avoid doing that in her presence. And if she decided to speak, she usually asked specific and intelligent questions. Tiberius almost hated to admit it, but he had become rather fond of the girl.

# CHAPTER FOURTEEN

"I NEED YOU TO KILL HIM," Sypheria said as she stretched across the padded loveseat in Tiberius's room. She popped a grape in her mouth and smiled at him.

"Why can't you poison him or have one of your guards do it?" He had been seated at his writing desk, penning a letter. He dipped his pen into the inkwell and left it there, pushed his papers aside, and stood. His eyes travelled the length of her body as he sat on the chair opposite. He poured himself a glass of wine, having dismissed his servants when the witch arrived. "Why do you need him killed, anyway?"

She nodded in the direction of the desk. "What were you writing?"

"Council business."

She sat straighter. "What council business?"

"Boring stuff. It'd be of no interest to you."

"As queen, any council business is of much interest to me." Her eyes narrowed.

Tiberius sighed and shifted in his seat. "Look, I'm not keeping anything from you. It's not important."

"Tell me."

"Fine, you wish to know so badly?" His face colored, a mixture of anger and embarrassment. "I'm learning to read and write." He averted his gaze and took a long sip from his goblet.

"You don't know how to read or write?" She sounded surprised.

"Why are you so shocked? I was a blacksmith. I can read a few words, but it was of no use until now."

"Hmm, I'm sure I'd have reconsidered your place on the council had I known that." She laughed and poured herself some wine.

"Which was a good reason for me not to tell you. Besides, lords know how to read and write, so I best learn."

"Indeed, they do."

"Speaking of which, when will I be receiving my lordship?"

"As soon as you do this one little thing for me."

"Killing the king is not a little thing, my queen."

She smiled at him and relaxed into the seat, one arm draped over the back.

"Sypheria, forgive me, but is killing him necessary?"

"It is if you want your lordship. He refuses to budge. He says I've given you enough power and he's starting to get suspicious. Rolamere's man said the king has been asking questions."

Tiberius frowned and took another gulp of wine.

"You question my reasons?"

"Well, perhaps he is asking questions because you're no longer playing the doting wife. Being queen is going to your head."

"How dare you?" she spat, then sat forward, sloshing wine into her lap.

"The guards talk." He passed her a piece of cloth. "So do the servants when they think no one is around. You'd be amazed at how often I go unnoticed."

She dabbed the wet patch of her dress. "Which is why you're

perfect for the job." She tossed the purple-stained rag aside and stared at him. "What have you heard?"

"You hammered a man's tongue to the floor of the throne room while it was still attached. He stayed there for hours before the nail was removed and he was allowed to see the healer. All because he called you a witch."

"That's not entirely true."

"No?"

"It was the entrance hall." She laughed. "Why do you look so worried?"

"I've called you that several times. Am I to lose my tongue, too?"

She smiled like a snake might smile at a mouse. When she slid over to sit on the chair beside him, his stomach lurched.

"When you say it, it's endearing. That cur said it as an insult, unaware I was within earshot. He's lucky to have escaped with his life, though I doubt the healer can save his tongue. Either way, he'll be keeping his mouth shut from now on."

Her thigh brushed against his and his mouth went dry, then she flattened a strand of hair near his ear and leaned closer.

"So, you'll do this for me? I need you," she purred.

He swallowed; the growing bulge between his legs made his breeches feel tight and uncomfortable. He considered asking for a favor in return, a different one to the lordship, but was too frightened. She knew what he wanted, and he knew she could easily kill him if he didn't do what she demanded. It wouldn't take much to sever the loose ties that made up their friendship, and he wasn't stupid enough to give her a reason to do so. He simply nodded.

When she leaned forward and pressed her lips against his, he closed his eyes and held his breath. "Thank you," she said, then got up and left, leaving his heart racing.

His breath rushed out in a whoosh, and he guzzled the rest of the wine, adjusting his still-hard cock through his breeches. He needed a whore, and he needed to get drunk. So drunk he could forget the conversation he'd had for a few hours, perhaps chase away the throbbing headache that had suddenly come upon him. He would spend the night at the pleasure house.

He called for his manservant.

"Ready my horse, I'm going out."

# CHAPTER FIFTEEN

Tiberius fumbled in the darkness as he tried to light the small torch. His hands shook as he struggled with the flint Sypheria had given him and dropped it.

"Horseshit!"

He crouched, keeping the torch close at hand, and felt around in the dirt until he found it. Taking a deep breath, he steadied his nerves, then stood. He held the torch near the wall and struck the flint against the stone. The bright sparks caught the pitch-soaked end, and a brilliant white flame erupted. He was amazed by its luminosity and the minimal heat it emitted. The witch had imbued the flint and torch with her magic, ensuring he would have no trouble lighting it in the damp tunnel and making sure it would stay lit for the duration of his trip. He angled the torch away from himself and started walking.

It would take him at least an hour to reach his destination, so the torch needed to last double that to ensure his safe and speedy return. He left the palace on horseback, claiming he was visiting the pleasure house. Once his task was completed, he would visit it, and should anyone ask, he would have a bevy of well-paid whores who would vouch for his whereabouts. He had left his horse tied up in the forest, far enough away from the tunnel's entrance not to rouse suspicion should anybody happen upon it but close enough for a hasty getaway.

Sypheria had revealed where the entrance was, about two miles from the palace behind a large hill in the middle of a nearby forest. It had taken him an hour to find the entrance; it was well hidden behind two boulders covered in shrubbery. That was the easy part. The witch had also explained the maze he would find under the palace, including each corridor and stairwell, but she refused to draw a map or allow him to write down any instructions in case he was caught.

He repeated the instructions in his head like a mantra, so he wouldn't get lost.

*Left-right-right-up-left-left.*
*Left-right-right-up-left-left.*
*Left-right-right-up-left-left.*

He would worry about getting out when he made it through.

His heart pounded against his ribcage, and the muscles in his back ached, his body stiff and tense. The torchlight only illuminated the tunnel a few lengths in front of him and when he heard a noise he flinched, almost dropping the torch. A mess of rats scurried passed, disturbed by the light. He turned to watch them go and relaxed when the tunnel returned to its haunting quiet, the only sounds were his footsteps and the occasional crackle of his torch flame.

The first intersection was covered in cobwebs. He waved the torch through, the silken webs disintegrating under the mild warmth of the flame. He went left, then transferred a small stick from his right pocket to his left. The six sticks would help him remember which stage of the tunnel he was up to.

*Right-right-up-left-left.*

He felt something crawl across his shoulder and down his chest and brought the light closer, then screamed when he saw a corpse spider! As big as his hand and the color of ash, the hairy, eight-legged body crawled across his tunic like it owned it. Tiberius dropped the torch and flapped his hands against his clothing, dancing on the spot as he knocked the creature off. It scurried across the ground and out of sight.

He grabbed the torch and waved it over the dirt but couldn't see where it went. Fingers of fear crept over him, and he patted his clothing down once more, then continued walking. Corpse spiders were never alone, so Tiberius took to checking the ceiling for more. He hated the things. Though not venomous, they had a nasty bite. They earned their name because they would live inside a fresh corpse and lay a hundred eggs, the hatchlings, and mother feasting on the flesh of the dead until there was nothing left but bone. He wondered if that meant he would come across a dead body in the tunnels.

*Right-right-up-left-left.*

Tiberius did his best to put them out of his mind; he had enough to worry about. He could see the next crossroad ahead.

THE STAIRS WERE a nightmare for him, spiraling upward in a tight circle. The steps were uneven, making him stumble and trip every few minutes. The narrowness of the corridor made him feel claustrophobic, and he was relieved when he finally reached the top. He was fortunate the magical flame emitted little smoke, or he might have spent the whole time coughing.

He had been walking for almost an hour and knew he was inside the castle walls. Sypheria had said the king's chambers were not far from the stairwell.

*Left-left.*

He turned and walked cautiously, fearing the guards would hear his footsteps despite the thick stone walls.

When he finally reached the end of the tunnel, he set his torch in the sconce to collect later and transferred the final stick to his left pocket. He approached the door as slowly as a moving cloud, allowing time for his eyes to adjust to the gloom as he walked away from his light source. He couldn't risk taking it with him, nervous the bright light might rouse the king from his slumber.

He felt like he was in a crypt, silent and dark, as he pressed his hands against the wall, searching for the lever that would open the door. He found it and pulled, cringing at the audible click. To him, it sounded like a hammer clanging against an anvil. He stood still for a long while, listening for any movement within. When he was satisfied he hadn't been heard, he pushed the fake wall open and stepped inside.

The doorway was set in a section of wall near the hearth and had been covered by a large tapestry. He slid out from behind it and let it settle back in place.

The room was warm, the fire had been stoked and fed enough to last the night. He stepped forward and looked around, his belly twisting in fear. King Cedric was asleep, lying on his back, his chest rising and falling. Tiberius grabbed a chair and carried it to the side of the bed and climbed up.

He withdrew the knife from the sheath that hung around his waist. The blade wasn't his; he had no idea whose it was, but he knew it would be found, still coated in the king's blood, during a search of the quarters of a man named Margrave, the royal treasurer. Tiberius wasn't sure what the man had done to Sypheria to deserve her wrath, but he knew when to ask questions and when to keep quiet.

He silently moved a chair next to the bed. He didn't need the chair, but he wasn't sure how adept the healers were at identifying the angles of cuts, and he wanted to make sure it looked like a man of regular height had committed the crime.

Before he lost his nerve, he quickly slashed the blade across the man's throat and flinched when the king's eyes shot open. A bubble of blood oozed from his mouth, and he grasped his bleeding neck with both hands. The cut went deep, severing the fattest veins, and blood flowed out in thick spurts like dark syrup. The king's hands did nothing to stop the deluge. He reached an arm out towards Tiberius, but the dwarf scrambled off the chair and moved away. Time seemed to crawl as he watched the man cling to the last remnants of life. Then the king took his last few raspy breaths and finally stopped moving.

Tiberius looked at Cedric's ashen face. His eyes stared, unseeing, at the ceiling, his mouth open in a silent scream. Blood pumped in a slow trickle between the king's crimson-stained fingers; the rusty smell made Tiberius queasy. It had taken all of five minutes to kill his king. Physically it was easy, but he was no assassin. He had never killed a man before and certainly never imagined he would do it like that, sneaking into his room as he slept like a baseborn coward. His stomach churned as bile clawed its way up his throat, and he was forced to swallow the acidic filth back down. Hot tears pricked the back of his eyes, and he let out a quiet sob, then backed away from the bed. He couldn't afford to fall apart now.

Footsteps beyond the door made the blood in his veins turn ice-cold, and a knot worked its way up his throat. He froze, a hand on the chair but ready to bolt down the tunnel if the knob turned.

*They'll find me. I could never outrun them.* Tall men with long legs waited on the other side of the door, armed and sworn to protect the man Tiberius had just killed. Creeping fear inched through his body, burrowing into his bones. He listened to the quiet words whispered between guards. *Shift change?* He concentrated on quieting his pounding heart as fear gnawed at his belly.

Finally, he heard a set of footsteps retreat. He moved the chair back to its place in front of the table, then disappeared back down the tunnel.

# CHAPTER SIXTEEN

Margrave's arrest was swift, and the trial was set for a few weeks later. The panel of judges was made up of the queen's council, Tiberius included, and two religious dignitaries of import. The proceedings were boring, and the men who had been paid off by Sypheria presented witness statements and evidence against the innocent man. Claims that the treasurer had been stealing from the crown came to light, and the accused was said to have killed the king to keep his secret. Since more than half the council was already controlled by the witch, the guilty verdict came quickly, and Margrave was sentenced to death by beheading.

Tiberius wondered if the information about the theft was true or if Sypheria had gotten Rolamere to tamper with the books. He didn't ask. It didn't matter; the witch did what she liked. She had become increasingly nasty over the past few months. He wondered, not for the first time, if the power had gone to her head. She seemed to be punishing all those who lovingly served her sister and the king before she was queen. There was a wall of tongues in the dungeons; a misspoken word and Sypheria would have her guards rip them out. Whispered rumors claimed she hammered the severed organs to the wall herself and had already amassed quite a collection.

WHEN MARGRAVE'S sentence was carried out, Tiberius waited amongst the townsfolk who called for the man's head. The sky was cloudy, hiding the sun and making the gray trees in the distance look like specters. The quiet afternoon exploded in angry shouts when the former treasurer was brought to the dais, and Tiberius felt a guilt-laced fear gnaw at his innards. The sack was removed, and the man was forced to his knees in front of the block. His red-rimmed eyes were in harsh contrast to his pale face as he scanned the hateful mob.

When the executioner picked up his axe, Tiberius couldn't watch. He allowed himself to be swallowed by the crowd and snuck off to the Dragon Forge Inn to drown his guilt in several mugs of pale ale.

# CHAPTER SEVENTEEN

Snow White had been understandably withdrawn since the death of her father. Wanting to do something to cheer her up, Tiberius visited the town toymaker. Together, they designed a doll suitable for the princess. He wanted something more extravagant than her usual dolls, and the man promised this one was the finest he had ever made.

It was crafted from clay, perfectly white and smooth. The man had painted bright blue eyes and ruby red lips on its little face, flanked by pink blushed cheeks. He had painstakingly glued strand after strand of hair to its head, made of the softest ebony silk the dwarf had ever felt, not that he had felt a lot. The hair was tied back with ribbons, and atop its little head sat a golden crown with clusters of colored glass in the front to look like jewels. The toymaker's wife had made the dress, a beautiful rose-gold gown. The bodice was fitted and covered with a fine layer of lace that ended at the waist, where the skirt billowed out. Underneath was a thick underskirt, complete with its own hoop. The top layers were gathered together in sections at the front with ruffles sewn in to keep the skirt in place. The look was finished with painted golden slippers.

The doll was exquisite, well worth the coin it had cost. Initially, Tiberius thought it exorbitant; he could've bought a cheap horse or a week with an even cheaper whore for that price. But holding the doll in his hands now, it exceeded his expectations.

IT WAS near the child's bedtime when the dwarf knocked on the princess's door, holding a white box tied with pink ribbon behind his back. At Snow's insistence, the nanny let him inside, muttering not to get her excited before bed.

They sat on the soft, thick rug in her playroom, and he watched as she excitedly undid the pink bow, removed the lid, and pulled out the tissue paper. When she first saw the doll, she gasped, then grinned, exposing her teeth, and Tiberius felt the tiniest twinge of happiness. It had been months since the king's death, and he hadn't seen anything but a gracious half smile plastered across her face. This one was genuine.

"You like it, then?"

"Oh, I love it, Uncle 'Berius. It's the best thing I've ever gotten."

She placed the box down, scurried over to give him a hug, then raced back to her spot on the rug and gently pulled the doll from the box. She ran her fingers along the ruffles of the dress, down the long silken black hair, and even upon the points of the crown.

"Is she a queen?" she asked.

"Maybe."

"I think she looks a bit like me if I was grown up."

"She does, indeed."

That was deliberate. He thought she would enjoy playing with a doll that resembled herself and pretend she was queen.

"I love it! Is it an early birthday gift? I'll be four soon, you know."

His cheeks flushed. He hadn't realized her birthday was so near. "I just wanted to cheer you up."

She smiled, never taking her eyes off the doll as she made it walk around the rug grandly.

"Thank you."

The poor girl's parents were dead, and he was partly responsible. Well, completely responsible in the case of the king, if he was being honest. Now, she had a stepmother who barely acknowledged her. A hell of a lot for a little girl to deal with. The doll wasn't going to solve her problems. Tiberius felt sympathy for her, but it was mostly an attempt to allay his guilt.

Though he couldn't forget what he had done, somehow, he was able to shut that part of himself away while he was with her. He was different with Snow. He wasn't someone's lackey or a dwarf. He was just 'Uncle 'Berius.'

The young woman returned and gathered Snow up from the rug. "Time for bed, Princess."

"Yes, nanny. Can Uncle 'Berius read me my bedtime story tonight?"

His stomach flipped.

Elia looked at him and guessing his predicament by the look on his face, did her best to dissuade Snow.

"Councilman Tiberius is an important man. I'm sure he has meetings to go to."

"Please, Uncle 'Berius." Snow clasped her hands together as she pleaded, her eyes wide.

How could he refuse her?

Elia rearranged the bed covers, then fetched a small book written for children.

"Um, sorry, Snow, I can't."

"Why not, Uncle?"

He shifted his weight from foot to foot, wondering if he

should make up an excuse. He decided it was best to tell her the truth to avoid having the same conversation another day. "I can't read, Princess."

"Oh? How come?"

"My dear child, Councilman Tiberius is busy. He probably never had time to learn."

"Oh." She looked disappointed, then her face lit up. "Why don't you learn with me? I have a tutor, you know. He says I'm to learn to read and write when I turn four, which is only a few weeks away. I don't mind starting earlier."

He felt heat spread across his face and cleared his throat. "I'm touched, Snow, but I..." Unsure how to finish his sentence, he ran a hand through his hair and averted his gaze.

"Sir, the tutor can be discrete, as can I," Elia said. "If it's something you'd like to do, don't let fear or shame stop you."

He looked up at her, stunned by her frankness. The way she smiled at him caused a familiar stirring in his loins.

"Oh please, Uncle, it'd be ever so much fun." Snow nodded.

"I'd be happy to have you join us for our bedtime story, Councilman." Elia patted the bed beside her and opened the book.

He cleared his throat and focused on the book in her lap as he sat down. "Please, call me Tiberius." Elia shifted position, and her thigh touched his, causing his heart to race. Time slowed when their eyes met, then Snow scrambled over to him, threw her arms around his neck, and the moment was over.

# CHAPTER EIGHTEEN

"It's all going well, don't you think?" Sypheria leaned close to a yellow rose and inhaled deeply. When he didn't answer, she turned to him, her brow creased with confusion.

"What's wrong? It's over now. You've done a great job, and no one suspects you."

The dwarf glanced around. They were walking through the palace gardens, and while there appeared to be no one within earshot, he was still nervous. That wasn't the only thing bothering him, however. Tiberius had only met Margrave in council meetings and held no feelings for him other than guilt from playing a part in an innocent man's death. He eased his conscience by telling himself he had had no choice, Sypheria made him do it. "It's been months since the beheading." He was trying to lead the conversation, afraid to ask outright for what he wanted.

"Patience, my dear." She smiled at him, then turned on her heel and continued her stroll through the garden.

A gnawing fear clawed at his gut, and he wracked his brain, trying to figure out where the feeling of apprehension was coming from.

"You're anxious for your lordship, is that it? Well, don't be. You shall have it. The treasurer's family has been removed from his estate in Brackenborough. I'll grant your lordship, and you can move in. It's a lovely house. Very big."

"That will please me," he said.

"Think of how many whores you can have hidden down there." She laughed.

He couldn't help but grin. Brackenborough was only a few hours' ride from the palace, and while he had never seen Margrave's estate, he had heard it was opulent, the grounds lush and plentiful.

"You'll have a full staff, too, of course," she continued, "and I might even raise your salary."

The niggle in his belly increased, and a thick lump formed in his throat. He realized the reason for his anxiety: she wanted something. She was being too nice for it not to be something huge, but he couldn't guess what it was. He stopped walking and glared at the back of her head until she turned around.

"Alright, Sypheria. What is it? What do you want?"

The witch slithered over to him like a seductive serpent, and a skitter of unease tingled its way down his spine. She smiled; her hot breath tickled his ear as she crouched to whisper. "I need you to kill Snow White."

# CHAPTER NINETEEN

Tiberius stood beside the bed and looked down at the angel that slept between fine silks and fluffy blankets. Her ebony hair sprawled across her face. He moved a curl away to expose her pale skin and rosy cheeks. She stirred and he pulled his hand back, smiling down at her. She opened her eyes and stretched her arms above her head, then grinned up at him.

"Uncle 'Berius, have you come to read me a story?" Her normally high voice was thick with sleep.

"No, Snow, it's too late for that."

"Oh." She sat up and pouted at him. "But you didn't read me one at bedtime."

"I know. I had an errand to run. A very important one."

He pulled his hand from behind his back. The moonlight glinted off the metal, and her eyes widened. He chuckled, then let the amulet drop, but kept hold of the chain so it swung back and forth.

"Is that for me?" Her excitement was palpable.

"It is." He sat on the edge of the bed and handed her the necklace so she could admire its fine craftsmanship. It was beautiful; he had made it himself.

A textured metal circle with tinted glasz as the centerpiece, a cerulean blue like the ocean to match her eyes. He had used up all the glasz on the witch's mirror, all except that piece, which he had kept in his pocket since the first day the dwarves had discovered it. His lucky piece. Now, it belonged to Snow. When Sypheria had imbued the rest of the glasz, this piece was there, too.

Across the glasz was a pentagram, an ancient sign of protection. The symbol wasn't enough, he knew. Which is why he had travelled for two days to an enchantress, one with old bones and a good heart, and had her imbue the amulet with a protection spell. The magic swirled around the glasz and made it glow.

"It's beautiful, Uncle. I'm so lucky."

A knot formed in his stomach. How innocent and pure she was, with no idea of the danger surrounding her. "You can only have it on one condition."

"What's that?"

He grabbed her hand and squeezed it gently. The gesture drew her eyes away from the jewel and to his. "You must promise me, with all your heart, that you'll never take it off."

"Alright, Uncle. I promise."

"There's more. You must wear it under your clothes."

"But why?" There was a whine in her tone she seldom used. "It's so beautiful; I want everyone to see it."

He shook his head. "I'm sorry, Snow, those are the rules. If the wrong people see it, they'll take it away from you. It's very important."

"Okay, but why?"

He sighed, then shifted forward to clasp the chain around her neck. The amulet hung low, and she tucked it under her nightgown. The glasz glowed bright blue for a moment, then faded. She stared at him with large, inquisitive eyes. He would have to tell her something.

"It's for protection, Snow. But it'll only work if you're wearing it or at least have it on your person."

"On my person?"

"Yes, like in your pocket or something."

"Oh." She giggled at the phrase. "But Uncle, I have guards to protect me."

"Yes, I know, but this is extra protection. Please wear it. It'll be our secret."

"What about nanny? She helps me dress and bathe."

"I trust your nanny. I'll tell her to keep our secret."

After months of studying alongside Snow and reading her bedtime stories, Tiberius had gotten close to both the princess and her nanny. After Snow had fallen asleep, he would thank Elia and say goodbye. As time went on, their goodbyes stretched out into actual conversations. Those few evenings a week eventually became the times Tiberius looked forward to the most.

Snow pressed her hand against the amulet through her shirt, her face serious. "I'll never take it off or show anyone. I promise, Uncle 'Berius."

He smiled and kissed her forehead, then his smile wavered. There was one more thing he wanted to tell her, but he wasn't sure he could.

She yawned and lay back down, a huge grin on her face.

"Snow?"

"Yes?" It was a sleep-induced mumble. He couldn't be sure she was still listening, but he said it anyway.

"I have to go away for a while. Maybe a long while. I just want you to know, no matter what anyone says, no matter what you hear … I love you."

Her only response was a small hum, so Tiberius stood and gently pulled the blankets up to her shoulders. "I'm sorry."

He thought it was better this way, no need to fuss, but it was something he had to say before he left, especially knowing they would never see each other again.

When he reached the door, he looked back one last time, then quietly left the room.

~

HE KNOCKED on Elia's room, which adjoined Snow's chambers. It was late, so he wasn't surprised when he didn't hear anything. He wanted to say goodbye, to tell her about the amulet, but didn't feel right sneaking into her room at night without permission.

*You just snuck into a princess's room.* Despite his sense of foreboding, he managed a quiet chuckle, then opened the door to the nanny's room.

"Elia?" he whispered as he shook her shoulder. She moaned and shifted, then sat upright.

"Is it Snow? Is something wrong?"

"No, no, nothing's wrong. Not exactly." He sat on the bed and took her hand.

"You've always been kind and trustworthy. I know you love Snow with all your heart."

"Of course. What's the matter?"

"I've had a protection amulet made for her, but she must wear it at all times for it to work."

"Is she in danger?" Elia's alarm was written on her sweet face.

"A princess is always in danger. I want to make sure she's safe because I have to go away." Tiberius didn't want to tell the woman too much and put her in danger, too. Best to just tell her the basics. She would never ask a council member what reason he had to leave, so he didn't have to make up a story about his absence.

"I wanted you to make sure she wears it and that you keep it a secret." He released her hand and stood. "Watch out for her."

"I always do, Councilor."

The way she addressed him sounded strange after being on a

first-name basis for months, ever since he started reading bedtime stories with her to Snow. He frowned.

"How long will you be away?"

He sighed, knowing it would be forever. He would never again see her warm smile or watch her lips as she sounded out the words he struggled with.

She seemed to know it was forever, too, her dark brown eyes bore into his. Throwing her blankets aside, she reached for his hand. She wore a rose-colored long chemise; though it covered everything, he could still see every curve of her body through the soft silk.

He longed to touch her but was convinced he had misinterpreted her gesture. He swallowed hard, his mouth suddenly dry, then took her hand without a word.

She pulled him onto the bed and pressed her mouth against his before he had had a chance to breathe. His hands groped at the ties of her nightgown, finally loosening the bow. He tore it open and slid his hand inside to cup one of her breasts. He was nervous like it was the first time he had bedded a woman. This wasn't like with the whores. Elia was soft and kind, smelled like flowers, and was writhing underneath him. No longer anxious, he kissed his way down her smooth, flawless body until his mouth found her center. He didn't leave the area until her hands grasped his hair, and her moans echoed around her small chamber.

Even after that, he was still surprised when she undid his laces and tugged his breeches off. He groaned when she snaked her hand between his legs and took hold of him, guiding him inside. With his weight pinning her to the mattress, he teased her first with shallow plunges, and when he finally sank fully into her warmth, he realized he had been wasting his life.

# CHAPTER TWENTY

THE DWARF'S horse sprinted through the forest as branches smacked Tiberius's face. He spurred the beast on; he needed to put as much distance between himself and Sypheria's men as possible. His breath was quick and heavy, and an icy fear clutched at his belly. If they caught him, Tiberius was sure Sypheria would kill him.

For a week, he had played along with the witch's plan to kill Snow, acting as dutifully as ever while he had secretly crafted the talisman and planned his escape. Rolamere had been tasked with directing suspicion of treason to a man who had served as king's guard to King Cedric, a man named Sir Felk. As hushed rumors wafted throughout the castle's underbelly, Tiberius had assumed time was on his side. He knew it was not when one of Sypheria's men saw him leaving Elia's chambers in the early hours. He had fled a short time later with his mallet and the few supplies he had managed to throw together.

Darkness undulated like dense smoke as he navigated his way around the forest, making it more difficult. He had briefly considered returning to the shack he had shared with the other dwarves and asking for help, perhaps hiding in the mines. They alone knew the way through the labyrinth of tunnels, he could hide there for weeks. Months, if need be. But that would put them in danger, it was possible they already were at risk just from having known him.

"I see him!" a guard called out, and Tiberius's heart leapt to his throat.

He swerved between large oaks, and the horse jumped over small shrubs nestled between the trees. There were more shouts from behind and the sound of galloping hooves from his left. More on his right. *They're going to surround me.* It was only a matter of time before he was caught.

An arrow whipped past his ear, then another struck his shoulder. He cried out and slumped to the side, barely managing to stay in the saddle. Suddenly, the horse stumbled forward, its front legs buckled underneath it, and the dwarf was flung from his seat, landing on the hard dirt. He looked at his horse; an arrow jutted out of its front leg. *What a waste.*

A black horse skidded to a stop in front of him, and he scrambled to his feet as its rider dismounted.

Tiberius thanked the gods he had strapped his mallet to his back rather than pack it in the saddlebags with his food and bedroll. He pulled it free and swung it at the man's legs. They snapped like twigs, and he fell to the ground, screaming in agony. The dwarf wasted no time and put an end to the man's wails by crushing his skull. The bone fragmented under the steel, shards spattering his boots. The sound reminded him of wet wood splintering. Dark inkblots of blood decorated the dirt and a piece of brain plopped softly in the leaf litter. He felt an acidic burn at the back of his throat, but he swallowed it down and turned to run. Horse legs kicked up dust on either side of him, blocking his escape, their riders aiming crossbows at his heart. Only now that he had paused did he feel the ache in his shoulder from the arrow. He gripped the handle of his mallet as a third rider joined the other two and looked down at the pulpy mess on the ground.

"Aye, dwarf. You've disappointed the queen." The man made a clicking noise with his tongue. "Now she'll have your head."

"I'd rather she gave me some instead."

"Drop the mallet, or the next thing you'll feel is an arrow in your balls."

"Fuck you." Tiberius spat.

One of the archers' directions shifted, now aiming at his groin. He swallowed hard but didn't drop his weapon despite the intense pain in his shoulder, which now radiated down his arm.

"The queen wants you alive, but she won't care if you're missing a piece or two."

One of the men dismounted and Tiberius turned to face him, but as he did, the leader spurred his horse forward and knocked the dwarf down. He lost his grip on the mallet as rough hands yanked him to his feet, then unceremoniously dumped him across the back of a horse behind its rider like a sack of potatoes. He winced as they trotted back to the palace, towards his doom.

# CHAPTER TWENTY-ONE

A DAMP SMELL permeated the air as a stygian gloom cloaked the sky beyond his cell window. A smudge of dark clouds floated across the moon, and for a while, his lodgings were almost blackened. Tiberius shifted on his cot; the rat-chewed blanket smelled of mold. Sleep wouldn't come easily tonight. Though he wasn't surprised, it was his last night. He had spent almost a month in the stinking cell until the verdict came. He was charged with colluding with Margrave for the king's murder and plotting against the queen and princess.

He was found guilty of treason and sentenced to death; his head was scheduled to be removed in a few short hours.

He thought about Snow and prayed to the Gods the amulet would be enough to save her. It sickened him to think her life was in danger simply because of who she was and the fact that her aunt, now step-mother, was a jealous and vengeful monster. The hateful woman wanted to abolish any reminder of her sister and feared any future claim Snow might make for the throne.

*Elia will watch over her.* As his thoughts drifted to the nanny, he was glad they had spent the night together but equally glad he hadn't shared her bed sooner. Tiberius wondered if she had slept with him only because she sensed she would never see him again. Perhaps it was better this way. If things were different, he might have fallen in love with her. Then Sypheria would have found out, putting Elia in danger, too. *At least she'll be safe.*

As dawn broke over the kingdom, the dwarf flitted in and out of sleep, restless and terrified.

~

"TIME TO GO," Rolamere said as he kicked Tiberius's cot.

He rolled over, not wanting to wake, then his fuzzy mind put his thoughts together, and he shot up in bed, eyes wide. His pulse thundered in his ears in time with the throb in his temples.

He was allowed to use the chamber pot; then a hessian sack was placed over him, resting heavily on his shoulders. It stunk of potatoes and manure and scratched his skin. He fought a wave of terror as he was marched to his finale. Even from the dungeons, he could hear the crowd outside as they cheered and demanded his head.

~

THE DWARF WAS LED to the wooden platform and positioned before the executioner. He wasn't given the opportunity to speak to the crowd; there was no point, his tongue had been ripped out days before, and his mouth still ached. The hood was removed, and he was forced onto his knees, head pushed down on the block, his neck settled into the groove. Tears spilled from the man's eyes down his clean-shaven face, and he squeezed them shut. He had argued with the guards at first, pleaded with the witch, that was when he had lost his tongue, now his struggle was over. This was his end. It wasn't fair, but no one ever said life was fair.

With his eyes closed, he didn't see the executioner pick up the axe, but he heard the roar of the crowd and felt a trickle of urine run down his leg. He prayed silently to any gods who would listen, but there was no one to help him. The executioner swung, and the dwarf's body dropped onto the dais with a thud.

Blood spattered the faces of those in the front row, and they squealed with gruesome delight. The head rolled for a few feet, and when it came to a stop, the crowd cheered. The dwarf was dead.

# CHAPTER TWENTY-TWO

Tiberius's heart raced, his muscles tight with fear and tension as the guards escorted him from his cell. He was afraid he would soil himself even though he had just used the chamber pot.

The crowd's blustering cheer would rise and fall like the sea during a storm, and he wondered if that meant he was getting close. Perhaps his lack of sleep caused his confusion because it felt as though he was being led further into the palace rather than outside. When they stopped walking, said confusion surpassed his fear. He knew they were in Sypheria's room. He had been in there enough times to know the smell of her perfume, the soft, cushioning feel of the rugs, even through his boots.

Rolamere yanked off his hood and he squinted for a moment at the brightness in the room before his gaze settled on the witch.

"Wine?" she asked as she poured him a chalice.

"Thank you."

He took the glass from her and took a tentative sip.

Sypheria laughed.

"You think I'd poison you?"

"You've used poison before," he shrugged.

"Just drink."

He took a long gulp and swallowed the liquid. If it was going to kill him, he decided he no longer cared. Beheading. Poisoning. What was the difference? When nothing happened, he passed the empty chalice back to her.

"Go look out the window."

He went to the window and looked down. Below, a large crowd had gathered around the wooden platform where the executioner stood waiting, axe in hand. His black hood, tunic, and breeches made him look especially menacing, even from this distance. Tiberius shivered when a cheer went up; then he saw the reason why. A dwarf was being led to the dais. He turned to look at Sypheria.

"Keep watching. It's only fair since the man's giving his life for you."

The pulse in his neck jumped under his skin as the guards removed the other dwarf's hood and forced his head on the block. The executioner swung his axe and separated his head from his body in one chop. It bounced on the dais, and a dark stain spread across the wood. A feral moan escaped his lips, and he heard Rolamere chuckle behind him. He stared at the head, his face close to the glass, squinting as though that would make his vision clearer. It wasn't anyone he knew.

*Where'd they find a dwarf who looked so similar to me?*

"You might be pleased to know your seven little friends came to see your beheading."

He looked at her, eyes wide with alarm, but she waved a hand and laughed.

"You look concerned. Why? I thought you hated them. You needn't worry, they were jostled so far towards the back they could barely see the dais. They believe you were up there, so I have no reason to kill them."

Tiberius felt some relief knowing the other dwarves weren't harmed. Despite his attitude towards them, they were good men.

"Leave us," she told Rolamere.

The queen's guard left, and Tiberius waited; his heart thumped against his ribs like a crazed animal trying to escape its cage. Was she showing him mercy? He didn't dare believe it, but why else would she find another dwarf who looked like him to take his place at the end of the axe?

"You've done me a kindness," he said, his tongue felt thick. He swallowed and wished he could have some more wine but wouldn't dare ask.

"That I have." She sat and gestured for him to do the same. He reluctantly sat across from her.

"Thank you, Your Majesty."

"Your Majesty? My, how formal. That has to be the first time you've called me that." She smiled, but there was no warmth in it. "Are you afraid of me, Tiberius?"

It was his turn to laugh. "Of course I am."

She leaned in closer and ran her tongue across her lip. For once, it did nothing to arouse him.

"You've no need to be. If you do as I wish."

A new fear squirmed in his belly, and he did his best not to look afraid. So, there it was. She hadn't shown him mercy for the friendship he thought they had forged. They were never friends; he was just another one of her puppets. They both sat in silence, staring at each other. She spoke first.

"I'm giving you one last chance for the friendship we had and for your loyal service. Kill Snow White, and all will be well. I'll forgive you for your rebellion and set you up in a nice house on the outskirts of the kingdom."

"Never." He stood and backed away, recalling the child's beautiful alabaster face as she laughed, how she would mimic his actions and follow him around the palace. The way she would hide her smirk if he mispronounced a word or how her face would light up after he had read a whole page correctly. "I could never harm Snow. I would rather be dead!"

"Are you sure?"

Her face darkened, and her features hardened into a scowl. Columns of light formed around her, white pillars from the sky burst through the palace ceiling as though it didn't exist.

Tiberius's stomach lurched, and he stumbled backwards, his eyes wide with fear.

"Please, Sypheria, don't kill me." He dropped to his knees as the storm of her power surged through the room.

The witch smiled and clapped. Dark whispers and a heavy fog swirled around the dwarf. Sweat ran down his back, and his head began to throb. His stomach lurched as savage wails escaped his mouth. A searing heat flooded his body almost as though his blood was boiling, a pulsing fire that thumped with each beat of his heart. He clasped his head in his hands as blood trickled from his ears, nose, and eyes, crimson ribbons streaking his face.

He saw the witch laugh through the pink hue created by his blood-filled orbs, but the sounds of her laughter were drowned out by his screams of agony. What felt like a lifetime of pain suddenly ended when his vision went black, and he collapsed on her plush rug.

# CHAPTER TWENTY-THREE

TIBERIUS AWOKE on a cold stone floor in a darkened room. He sat up, surprised but glad to be alive, and rubbed his sore joints as his eyes adjusted to the gloom. Aside from some stiffness, he sustained no injuries.

He felt no breeze but could make out a slowly billowing mist surrounding him with a hint of light behind it. He stood and walked towards it, reaching out so as not to bump into any walls, and was surprised when he couldn't step through the fog. He moved further along, feeling with his hands, but they would barely penetrate the smoke wall before him. It was as though the mist prevented him from leaving the confines of that small space. He heard nothing but his own heartbeat and heavy breathing. Those sounds alone increased his anxiety. Frantically, he rushed along the misty prison, searching for a door, a window, anything, but his hands met nothing but the strange fog.

After what felt like hours, Tiberius collapsed, disorientated, in a heap on the hard ground. With barely any light piercing the mist, he had become dizzy and confused. He hugged his knees to his chest and wept, rocking back and forth like a frightened child.

Time became meaningless. Had it been hours or days? When

a large oval of light appeared, Tiberius wasn't sure if it was real. The mist cleared, and the witch appeared in the window, smiling down at him. He climbed to his feet and approached her. As he drew near, his confused mind pieced together what he saw, and he cried out in anguish. Beyond the evil queen, he saw the opulence of her royal chamber, the silken bedspread, the tapestry he had always thought was so hideous, and he realized it was not a window at all but the back of the very mirror he had made for her. He bashed his fists against the glasz, knowing he could never break it, and sobbed when she laughed.

"How?" he asked. "How did I get here?"

"A gift from Daramond the Displacer, when I ate his heart," the witch said.

Tiberius recalled the fight in Sypheria's chambers; the sorcerer had displaced the guard from inside the room to outside, without lifting a finger.

"Let me out, please."

"I don't think so. I'm not even sure I know how."

"Please," he said, his forehead resting on his side of the glasz. "You can't leave me here."

"Oh, but I can, and I shall. This is your punishment, little man, for your betrayal. You are henceforth banished to this horrible nothingness." Her lips curled into an evil smile. "And you'll continue to do my bidding as I see fit." She waved her hand, and a series of other mirrors appeared in the mist, some showing the inside of other rooms, others showing areas in the surrounding forests or the township. In a few, he recognized the native brush of Kingdom Valence, so different from the forests of Woodhaven. He saw the kingdom of Whitefall; the ground blanketed in snow, the mountain peaks touching the sky. There were places shown in other mirrors he didn't recognize. He ran to the ones where he saw people and banged his fists against them, screaming at the occupants on the other side for help.

"They can't see or hear you, of course, but you can see and

hear them. You'll be able to watch them as often as I require. And tell me all their schemes and secrets."

The portal to his right shimmered, and he ran to it. It displayed a view into Snow White's room. She sat on a fluffy rug with her nanny, playing with some dolls. Elia was holding the doll he had given Snow months before, and Snow held one that she had bent at the knee.

*"Hello, my lord, might I have this dance?"* Elia asked.

*"Of course, Princess, you are very beautiful,"* Snow said.

*"And you are the handsomest lord I've ever seen,"* Elia said, and they both giggled.

It made him feel as though someone had ripped out his heart and fed it to a pack of hellhounds.

"Snow," he wept, his hand slapping against the mirror. She didn't look up. He hoped the witch would never find out how he felt about Elia, or she would be dead. Or worse.

Suddenly, the mirrors were replaced with Sypheria's reflection, cackling like a crone, and despite her undeniable beauty, for once, Tiberius saw she was actually ugly. Cold and rotten on the inside, she was more evil than he ever could have imagined. He wondered how he could have ever harbored fantasies of sharing her bed and perhaps even ruling beside her.

He thought about what his life might have been like if he had only stayed the disgruntled blacksmith, working alongside his fellow dwarves, living in that stinky, cramped, but safe cabin.

As quickly as they appeared, the mist billowed around the room, and the grey fog sucked away each portal, obscuring his view. He turned to the lone remaining mirror and seethed at Sypheria.

"You can't touch her. I had an enchantress cast a protection spell on her."

"Spells can be broken," she said.

"Not this one."

"Even so, all magic runs out eventually. I'll need to learn

patience." Her smile once sent shivers through his groin; now, it turned his stomach and filled his veins with ice-cold fear.

"You evil bitch!" He ran at her with all his strength, determined to break through, but crashed against the unbreakable glasz and was knocked to the floor.

"Evil? Oh, but you have your life, just as you requested."

"I won't do it," he spat. "I won't help you. I'll no longer be your pawn."

"I think you will," she said and licked her lips.

"I'll not spy on people for you. I refuse. What can you do to me here? If I can't die, what's to be afraid of?" He laughed, thinking he had won at least this small victory.

"Hmm, very well." She waved her hand and spoke a few words under her breath.

Her face shimmered as a black cloud crossed the mirror, darkening its surface, then covered it completely. The mist swirled around him, becoming thicker and darker until it blacked out the dim light that had previously filtered through from the portals.

It was like before, only worse. There was no sound other than those his body made and no light at all, just pure blackness. He walked forward, his hands held in front of him, to where he thought the mirror would be but felt nothing. He kept walking. He was sure he hadn't changed direction, but he still never found the edge. Not even the misty wall that had blocked his path earlier.

"Is this it? Is this all there is?" His echo was so loud it hurt his ears. *If there's an echo, there must be walls.* But it didn't matter how far he walked; he couldn't find any. He sat and cried, and though exhausted, sleep refused to find him. *Perhaps if I can't die, maybe I can't sleep either. Am I alive or dead? Am I still me?*

～

TIBERIUS DIDN'T KNOW how much time had passed when the large oval mirror finally reappeared. He crawled forward and waited, his heart in his throat. When the mist cleared, and Sypheria smiled down at him, he clasped his hands together and pleaded.

"Please don't do that again. I beg of you." His voice was raspy from not being used for so long.

She laughed.

"Snow, let me see her."

"If I do, are you going to be more cooperative?"

"Yes, I will. Just promise not to leave me here alone in the dark like that again."

"Very well." She smiled and waved her hand.

He turned slowly to face the portal that looked into Snow's room. He wondered how much time had gone by. Had it been years? Would she look different? When the mist cleared, and he saw Snow taking a lesson with her tutor, he frowned and turned to the witch.

"I don't understand; she looks the same."

"What don't you understand, Dwarf?"

"I thought she'd look older, changed."

"How much time do you think has passed?"

He shrugged. "A year, at least."

Sypheria laughed. She laughed so hard she clasped her hands to her belly and bent forward. When she had stopped and caught her breath, she actually had a tear in her eye from the strain of her giggling. "Oh, Tiberius, it's only been a month. You poor thing." Her words held no sympathy.

Tiberius turned back to Snow; all defiance drained away. He would do the witch's bidding, he realized. Better to answer her and at least get to watch the ones he loved live on than to sink into the abyss of madness, the purgatory she had created for him. Snow's portal clouded over, and he turned back to Sypheria. The witch wanted his attention, and he would give it to her. He would give her whatever she wanted, just like before.

Sypheria moved to the mirror, her hips sashaying and her breasts jiggling in a way that would have tightened his breeches in the past but now filled him with a cold, hard hatred. She removed her choker, a thin black ribbon adorned with a single onyx jewel, and loosened her hair, letting it fall around her shoulders like black silk. She trailed her fingertips down her collarbone.

"Now, Magic Mirror, tell me how beautiful I am."

Tiberius tilted his head as he studied her face, a sneer curling the corners of his mouth. "Hmm. I think I see a wart."

# GRIMM'S FAIRY TALES

## THE ORIGINAL SNOW-WHITE AND THE SEVEN DWARFS

IT WAS the middle of winter, and the snow-flakes were falling like feathers from the sky, and a Queen sat at her window working, and her embroidery-frame was of ebony. And as she worked, gazing at times out on the snow, she pricked her finger, and there fell from it three drops of blood on the snow. And when she saw how bright and red it looked, she said to herself, "Oh that I had a child as white as snow, as red as blood, and as black as the wood of the embroidery frame!" Not very long after she had a daughter, with a skin as white as snow, lips as red as blood, and hair as black as ebony, and she was named Snow-white. And when she was born the Queen died.

After a year had gone by the King took another wife, a beautiful woman, but proud and overbearing, and she could not bear to be surpassed in beauty by any one. She had a magic looking-glass, and she used to stand before it, and look in it, and say, "Lookingglass upon the wall, Who is fairest of us all?"

And the looking-glass would answer, "You are fairest of them all." And she was contented, for she knew that the looking-glass spoke the truth.

Now, Snow-white was growing prettier and prettier, and

when she was seven years old she was as beautiful as day, far more so than the Queen herself. So one day when the Queen went to her mirror and said, "Looking-glass upon the wall, Who is fairest of us all?" it answered,

"Queen, you are full fair, 'tis true, But Snow-white fairer is than you."

This gave the Queen a great shock, and she became yellow and green with envy, and from that hour her heart turned against Snow-white, and she hated her.

And envy and pride like ill weeds grew in her heart higher every day, until she had no peace day or night. At last she sent for a huntsman, and said, "Take the child out into the woods, so that I may set eyes on her no more. You must put her to death, and bring me her heart for a token."

The huntsman consented, and led her away; but when he drew his cutlass to pierce Snow-white's innocent heart, she began to weep, and to say, "Oh, dear huntsman, do not take my life; I will go away into the wild wood, and never come home again." And as she was so lovely the huntsman had pity on her, and said, "Away with you then, poor child"; for he thought the wild animals would be sure to devour her, and it was as if a stone had been rolled away from his heart when he did not put her to death. Just at that moment a young wild boar came running by, so he caught and killed it, and taking out its heart, he brought it to the Queen for a token. And it was salted and cooked, and the wicked woman ate it up, thinking that there was an end of Snow-white.

Now, when the poor child found herself quite alone in the wild woods, she felt full of terror, even of the very leaves on the trees, and she did not know what to do for fright. Then she began to run over the sharp stones and through the thorn bushes, and the wild beasts after her, but they did her no harm. She ran as long as her feet would carry her; and when the evening drew near she came to a little house, and she went inside to rest.

Everything there was very small, but as pretty and clean as possible. There stood the little table ready laid, and covered with a white cloth, and seven little plates, and seven knives and forks, and drinkingcups. By the wall stood seven little beds, side by side, covered with clean white quilts. Snow-white, being very hungry and thirsty, ate from each plate a little porridge and bread, and drank out of each little cup a drop of wine, so as not to finish up one portion alone. After that she felt so tired that she lay down on one of the beds, but it did not seem to suit her; one was too long, another too short, but at last the seventh was quite right; and so she lay down upon it, committed herself to Heaven, and fell asleep.

When it was quite dark, the masters of the house came home. They were seven dwarfs, whose occupation was to dig underground among the mountains.

When they had lighted their seven candles, and it was quite light in the little house, they saw that some one must have been in, as everything was not in the same order in which they left it.

The first said, "Who has been sitting in my little chair?" The second said, "Who has been eating from my little plate?" The third said, "Who has been taking my little loaf?" The fourth said, "Who has been tasting my porridge?" The fifth said, "Who has been using my little fork?" The sixth said, "Who has been cutting with my little knife?" The seventh said, "Who has been drinking from my little cup?"

Then the first one, looking round, saw a hollow in his bed, and cried, "Who has been lying on my bed?" And the others came running, and cried, "Some one has been on our beds too!" But when the seventh looked at his bed, he saw little Snow-white lying there asleep. Then he told the others, who came running up, crying out in their astonishment, and holding up their seven little candles to throw a light upon Snow-white.

"O goodness! O gracious!" cried they, "what beautiful child is this?" and were so full of joy to see her that they did not wake her, but let her sleep on. And the seventh dwarf slept with his comrades, an hour at a time with each, until the night had passed.

When it was morning, and Snow-white awoke and saw the seven dwarfs, she was very frightened; but they seemed quite friendly, and asked her what her name was, and she told them; and then they asked how she came to be in their house.

And she related to them how her step-mother had wished her to be put to death, and how the huntsman had spared her life, and how she had run the whole day long, until at last she had found their little house.

Then the dwarfs said, "If you will keep our house for us, and cook, and wash, and make the beds, and sew and knit, and keep everything tidy and clean, you may stay with us, and you shall lack nothing."

"With all my heart," said Snow-white; and so she stayed, and kept the house in good order. In the morning the dwarfs went to the mountain to dig for gold; in the evening they came home, and their supper had to be ready for them. All the day long the maiden was left alone, and the good little dwarfs warned her, saying, "Beware of your step-mother, she will soon know you are here. Let no one into the house." Now the Queen, having eaten Snow-white's heart, as she supposed, felt quite sure that now she was the first and fairest, and so she came to her mirror, and said,

"Looking-glass upon the wall, Who is fairest of us all?" And the glass answered, "Queen, thou art of beauty rare, But Snow-white living in the glen With the seven little men Is a thousand times more fair."

Then she was very angry, for the glass always spoke the truth, and she knew that the huntsman must have deceived her, and that Snow-white must still be living. And she thought and thought how she could manage to make an end of her, for as long as she was not the fairest in the land, envy left her no rest. At last she thought of a plan; she painted her face and dressed herself like an old peddler woman, so that no one would have known her. In this disguise she went across the seven mountains, until she came to the house of the seven little dwarfs, and she knocked at the door and cried, "Fine wares to sell! fine wares to sell!" Snow-white peeped out of the window and cried, "Good-day, good woman, what have you to sell?" "Good wares, fine wares," answered she, "laces of all colors"; and she held up a piece that was woven of variegated silk.

"I need not be afraid of letting in this good woman," thought Snow-white, and she unbarred the door and bought the pretty lace.

"What a figure you are, child!" said the old woman, "come and let me lace you properly for once." Snow-white, suspecting nothing, stood up before her, and let her lace her with the new lace; but the old woman laced so quickly and tightly that it took Snow-white's breath away, and she fell down as dead.

"Now you have done with being the fairest," said the old woman as she hastened away.

Not long after that, towards evening, the seven dwarfs came home, and were terrified to see their dear Snow-white lying on the ground, without life or motion; they raised her up, and when they saw how tightly she was laced they cut the lace in two; then she began to draw breath, and little by little she returned to life.

When the dwarfs heard what had happened they said, "The old peddler woman was no other than the wicked Queen; you must beware of letting any one in when we are not here!" And when the wicked woman got home she went to her glass and said, "Lookingglass against the wall, Who is fairest of us all?"

And it answered as before, "Queen, thou art of beauty rare, But Snow-white living in the glen With the seven little men Is a thousand times more fair." When she heard that she was so struck with surprise that all the blood left her heart, for she knew that Snow-white must still be living.

"But now," said she, "I will think of something that will be her ruin." And by witchcraft she made a poisoned comb. Then she dressed herself up to look like another different sort of old woman. So she went across the seven mountains and came to the house of the seven dwarfs, and knocked at the door and cried, "Good wares to sell! good wares to sell!" Snow-white looked out and said, "Go away, I must not let anybody in." "But you are not forbidden to look," said the old woman, taking out the poisoned comb and holding it up. It pleased the poor child so much that she was tempted to open the door; and when the bargain was made the old woman said, "Now, for once, your hair shall be properly combed." Poor Snow-white, thinking no harm, let the old woman do as she would, but no sooner was the comb put in her hair than the poison began to work, and the poor girl fell down senseless.

"Now, you paragon of beauty," said the wicked woman, "this is the end of you," and went off. By good luck it was now near evening, and the seven little dwarfs came home. When they saw Snow-white lying on the ground as dead, they thought directly that it was the step-mother's doing, and looked about, found the poisoned comb, and no sooner had they drawn it out of her hair than Snow-white came to herself, and related all that had passed. Then they warned her once more to be on her guard, and never again to let any one in at the door.

And the Queen went home and stood before the looking-glass and said, "Looking-glass against the wall, Who is fairest of us all?" And the looking-glass answered as before, "Queen, thou art of beauty rare, But Snow-white living in the glen With the seven little men Is a thousand times more fair."

When she heard the looking-glass speak thus she trembled and shook with anger. "Snow-white shall die," cried she, "though it should cost me my own life!" And then she went to a secret lonely chamber, where no one was likely to come, and there she made a poisonous apple. It was beautiful to look upon, being white with red cheeks, so that any one who should see it must long for it, but whoever ate even a little bit of it must die. When the apple was ready she painted her face and clothed herself like a peasant woman, and went across the seven mountains to where the seven dwarfs lived. And when she knocked at the door Snow-white put her head out of the window and said, "I dare not let anybody in; the seven dwarfs told me not to." "All right," answered the woman; "I can easily get rid of my apples else-where. There, I will give you one." "No," answered Snow-white, "I dare not take anything."

"Are you afraid of poison?" said the woman, "look here, I will cut the apple in two pieces; you shall have the red side, I will have the white one." For the apple was so cunningly made, that all the poison was in the rosy half of it. Snow-white longed for the beautiful apple, and as she saw the peasant woman eating a piece of it she could no longer refrain, but stretched out her hand and took the poisoned half. But no sooner had she taken a morsel of it into her mouth than she fell to the earth as dead. And the Queen, casting on her a terrible glance, laughed aloud and cried, "As white as snow, as red as blood, as black as ebony! This time the dwarfs will not be able to bring you to life again." And when she went home and asked the looking-glass, "Looking-glass against the wall, Who is fairest of us all?" at last it answered, "You are the fairest now of all." Then her envious heart had peace, as much as an envious heart can have.

The dwarfs, when they came home in the evening, found Snow-white lying on the ground, and there came no breath out of her mouth, and she was dead.

They lifted her up, sought if anything poisonous was to be found, cut her laces, combed her hair, washed her with water and wine, but all was of no avail, the poor child was dead, and remained dead. Then they laid her on a bier, and sat all seven of them round it, and wept and lamented three whole days. And then they would have buried her, but that she looked still as if she were living, with her beautiful blooming cheeks.

So they said, "We cannot hide her away in the black ground."

And they had made a coffin of clear glass, so as to be looked into from all sides, and they laid her in it, and wrote in golden letters upon it her name, and that she was a King's daughter. Then they set the coffin out upon the mountain, and one of them always remained by it to watch. And the birds came too, and mourned for Snow-white, first an owl, then a raven, and lastly, a dove.

Now, for a long while Snow-white lay in the coffin and never changed, but looked as if she were asleep, for she was still as white as snow, as red as blood, and her hair was as black as ebony.

It happened, however, that one day a King's son rode through the wood and up to the dwarfs' house, which was near it. He saw on the mountain the coffin, and beautiful Snow-white within it, and he read what was written in golden letters upon it. Then he said to the dwarfs, "Let me have the coffin, and I will give you whatever you like to ask for it." But the dwarfs told him that they could not part with it for all the gold in the world. But he said, "I beseech you to give it me, for I cannot live without looking upon Snow-white; if you consent I will bring you to great honor, and care for you as if you were my brethren."

When he so spoke the good little dwarfs had pity upon him and gave him the coffin, and the King's son called his servants and bid them carry it away on their shoulders. Now it happened that as they were going along they stumbled over a bush, and with the shaking the bit of poisoned apple flew out of her throat. It was not long before she opened her eyes, threw up the cover of the coffin, and sat up, alive and well.

"Oh dear! where am I?" cried she. The King's son answered, full of joy, "You are near me," and, relating all that had happened, he said, "I would rather have you than anything in the world; come with me to my father's castle and you shall be my bride." And Snow-white was kind, and went with him, and their wedding was held with pomp and great splendor.

But Snow-white's wicked step-mother was also bidden to the

feast, and when she had dressed herself in beautiful clothes she went to her looking-glass and said, "Looking-glass upon the wall, Who is fairest of us all?"

The looking-glass answered, "O Queen, although you are of beauty rare, The young bride is a thousand times more fair." Then she railed and cursed, and was beside herself with disappointment and anger. First she thought she would not go to the wedding; but then she felt she should have no peace until she went and saw the bride. And when she saw her she knew her for Snow-white, and could not stir from the place for anger and terror.

For they had ready red-hot iron shoes, in which she had to dance until she fell down dead.

**THE END**

# ACKNOWLEDGEMENTS

I'd like to thank my mum, Anna, who I think might be my biggest fan and is a continual pillar of support. Thank you to my beta reader, Meagan Curtis, and to my cat, Tyrion (yes, named after the GoT character), who was my constant companion, sitting on my desk and leaning against my laptop as I wrote. Slightly less thanks go to my other cat, Delphia, and my chihuahua, Ren, who mainly distracted me.

I am extremely grateful to my editors and proofreaders, Sarah Chorn, A.M Rycroft, Ayelén Caparra, and the team at Epic Publishing.

I would especially like to thank the Brother's Grimm for their fairy tales that have inspired writers for hundreds of years and will continue to do so, for many years to come.

I am deeply indebted to my fellow readers and lovers of fairy tale retellings. I hope you found this story worthy of your time and will read more of my work.

# ABOUT THE AUTHOR

R.A. Goli is an Australian writer of horror, fantasy, and speculative short stories. Her interests include reading, gaming, the occasional cemetery walk, and annoying her chihuahua, and two cats. As a child, her imaginary friends were two werewolf cubs who lived under her bed. When she was twelve years old, she tried to summon Sid Vicious with a home-made Ouija board.

He didn't respond.

Check out her numerous publications, including her collection of short stories, *Unfettered*, at https://ragoliauthor.word press.com, where you can sign up for her newsletter to get free short stories, updates, and more, or stalk her on Facebook at https://www.facebook.com/RAGoliAuthor.

# EXCERPT FROM DEMONS & RAMEN

## BY A.M. LOWEECEY

The sign's fat black letters proclaimed in Italian and English:

**Danger**
**Keep Out**
**By Order of the Pontifical Commission for Sacred**
**Archeology.**

It was crowned with the official Vatican seal, too. Maybe their pompous crap worked on tourists.

I slung my leather messenger bag across my back and scaled the chain-link fence surrounding the excavation. My feet hit broken cobblestones on the other side with a puff of stone dust. I brushed at my black slacks and shirt. They were the wrong clothes for crashing a closed dig, but I hadn't confronted an entity yet who didn't at least pause at the sight of the Roman collar. Most of them pissed their ectoplasmic pants. We had… used to have… a reputation, Xavier and me.

There wasn't another living person in sight in this obscure corner of Rome on this muggy August evening. Exactly what I'd wanted.

In the three weeks since Xav died, I'd scoured every ruined cemetery and archaeological dig in Vatican City for his murderer, the demon who forced Xav to eat a bullet. My rage and hate drew the scaly, red-assed bastards out like stray dogs scenting ripe meat. I slammed every one I could find back to Hell. So far none of them had claimed responsibility, but demons lie.

Any other entities wanting to play High Noon with the left-over Kaine got the same treatment.

Simply put, this was The Plan.

I clambered over broken stone which had once been the foundation of this ninth-century church. Tree roots had done more damage to it than a millennium's weather. Shame. I could see the remains of carvings on some of the smaller pieces of stone. Probably from the columns.

Beneath the sticky breeze I sensed a strong, hidden presence. Last night, I'd sensed it even through the fog of two bottles of grappa—I was pretty sure I'd finished off the second one; things got hazy around midnight—the presence hidden here hit me like a two-by-four. Good thing the streets in Rome were narrow. I'd needed a wall to keep me vertical. Keep me heading back to the Friary, too. I had to be sober to challenge something with such strength. As sober as I got these days, anyway.

So. I set my messenger bag on a stable stone and unbuckled the straps. Never mess with a successful ritual. Ask any athlete. My ritual always began by fanning open the bag's three compartments. I'd arranged the contents to give me easy access to the essentials in case things went south.

Salt. Holy water. Silver-and-cedar flute.

I straightened, got my balance, and closed my eyes. Breathing in a slow, even rhythm, I shut out the world one piece at a time. The sound of the wind faded first. Then the rumble of distant traffic. The smells of gasoline and garbage. The light on my face from the setting sun.

When I didn't hear my heartbeat or feel my breathing, I

reached inside myself. My hands cupped the power visible only to me, Xavier, and any otherworldly creatures in the vicinity. I gathered its pulsing energy which flowed through me like a second bloodstream and flung it outward like I was snapping a tablecloth over a banquet table.

I opened my eyes as a shimmering blanket of blue and white, the colors of shadows on snow, settled over the entire dig.

And I pinpointed it twenty yards northeast. Only one entity… ghost… demon… something. The magical wards on some kind of prison tomb were so strong they camouflaged whatever it was they imprisoned.

I scooped up the messenger bag and headed to the northeast end of the dig. A four-foot square pit butted up against the fence in the far corner. More dirt. Why the hell hadn't I worn jeans?

Holding the bag with one hand and steadying myself with the other, I skidded down a root-studded slope into shadows.

A mostly solid stone crypt door was hidden beneath the tips of the roots. I studied the layout of the ruin. If the pillars on the southern side had been the entrance, this crypt had been beneath the altar or sacristy. I wouldn't want to change into Mass vestments over a bunch of rotting corpses, but in those days rich folks seemed to think being buried under a church gave them a "Get Out of Purgatory Free" card.

Dirt obscured the writing carved into the seal across the crypt. I brushed most of it away and used my thumbnail on the rest. The one time I could've used a flashlight… I squinted and made out Old Latin and Cyrillic. Interesting. Why Cyrillic? The words across the seal informed me they kept the entity on the other side imprisoned in the name of the Blessed Trinity and His Holiness Pope—I scraped more—Nicholas III.

I whistled. Imprisoned more than seven hundred years and still powerful enough for me to sense it through a two-day drunk.

Couldn't banish it until I knew what it was. I took my flask of holy water in my left hand and palmed a vial of salt in my right. I pictured the shield of Michael the Archangel, my patron, the way Rubens painted it: golden flames on silver, burning with cold fire. My power rose with the image and a gold-silver-snow-shadow barrier bloomed in front of me.

When Xav and I discovered our power as kids, we'd grab the biggest sticks we could find and bash each other's shields until they shivered and dissolved back into our skin. Grandmère caught us the third time and threw us into the pond. When we squelched out we explained, sort of. She marched us into the parlor, opened the glass-front bookcase, and took out a volume of French sermons nobody ever read. She opened it and showed us the diary hidden in a hole cut into the pages. In it her great-aunt drew the shield and glowing spheres she could create, and only on her deathbed told her great-niece about the diary.

We searched in France for her ancestry and found an ancestor who'd been exorcist to a Pope. But then the Inquisition happened and the grandson of said ancestor fled to Canada. Word of mouth in our family garbled over the centuries insisted we were blessed, not cursed, since we were all devout Catholics. Grandmère wasn't surprised we became priests.

A tickle of bluish green, the color of a deep river, explored my shield. So whatever was in the crypt sensed my presence. The first verse of *"Noel Nouvelet,"* my mental shield, played in my head. And counterpoint to it I heard a whisper of a tune from whatever was in the crypt. Damned thing was reading me. I followed the melody to its source and the riverlike incursion from it changed from a tickle to a stab.

Eh, screw it. Either I was stronger than it, or I wasn't. I didn't give a shit either way.

I picked up a piece of masonry, drew a cross on it with the holy water, and slammed it into the seal.

The doors shattered. I ducked wood shrapnel, covering my

bag. Injuries to my back could be repaired easier than injuries to my tools.

The air behind the shrapnel didn't reek of the usual hate-evil-violence cocktail. Hate was there—nothing smelled more acrid, not even a wendigo after its latest meal. But this trapped air smelled more of rivers and snow and museums—a bizarre mix of vitality and decay.

The thing leaped into the sun and flung up its arm to shield its eyes. After seven hundred years, its body was nothing more than papery skin clinging to a withered skeleton. Its mushroom-white hair fell past its hips. Shreds of what used to be a dress hung on its—her—body.

I tried Italian first. "Who are you?"

She jerked around, breathing like she'd raced over the Seven Hills. I tried the same question in Latin.

Her emaciated claw—hand—shot forward and grabbed my shirt. "Who are you? Are you a holy man?"

She spoke in a jumble of Late Latin and what sounded like Russian. I caught the gist of it. Good thing I'd paid attention in specialized history classes.

"I am," I answered in Late Latin. "Do you want—"

With a shriek she clawed my face. I shoved her away and began a banishing spell I'd learned in New Orleans. Her shrieks turned into curses; some things had no language barrier. I flung salt in a cross pattern at her.

She leaped to the top of the crypt ruins like she was Spring-Heeled Jack. Her gray rags fluttered in the wind before blending into the stone. She'd camouflaged herself to match them, or she was a super-powered shape-shifter.

"I'll be da—" My teeth clicked shut before I said something irreparable.

The sounds of evening traffic roared around me. The garbage in the nearby alley stunk up the place once more. The heat clung to my face. I touched my cheek.

"Aah—" My hand came away dripping blood. "You're welcome, you bitch!"

*Sorry, Xavier. What about some help from On High, eh? The next crypt I open might be hiding a pissed-off mama bear demon protecting her spawn.*

Great. It had only taken me three weeks from burying Xavier to begin talking to him like he was my Heavenly tech support.

I repacked my bag and headed to the Friary. This time of day, everyone would be teaching and I could repair the creature's damage without a lot of concerned-but-nosy questions.

As I walked back, a hand pressed to my cheek, I wondered: What exactly was the creature? Xavier'd always been quicker at research. He'd have nailed its nature down in an hour.

Shit, I was supposed to stop thinking about him. I was supposed to be kicking demon ass and shoving ghosts and haunts and other assorted spirits to meet their Judgment. Whether they wanted to or not. How the hell else was I going to deal with what happened to Xavier?

But I knew the answer.

I couldn't do this without Xav. It'd just taken me three weeks to admit it.

Well, then.

~

To get your copy of *Demons & Ramen*, visit the Epic Publishing website (www.epic-publishing.com/books) or go to your favorite bookseller.

To keep up to date on all of Epic Publishing newest releases, follow our blog (www.epic-publishing.com/blog) or join our Epic News List (www.epic-publishing.com/subscribe).

www.ingramcontent.com/pod-product-compliance
Lightning Source LLC
Chambersburg PA
CBHW010343170726
48283CB00009B/2938